There was a renewed storm of flying lead

The Executioner popped up, triggered a burst as the gunners kept charging. Bolan knew he was fast running out of time to call the shots in there, and he needed Broadwater to hold back the cavalry, now more than ever.

Bolan palmed his radio. "I'm still in the picture, Broadwater."

"I just tagged one coming out of the store!"

"Call your boss, do whatever it takes, but don't let SWAT storm this place. I've got women and children, unscathed...."

"I read you, loud and clear. I'll do what I can."

"Make it happen."

Bolan was up and searching for more targets.

MACK BOLAN ®
The Executioner

DON PENDLETON'S
THE EXECUTIONER®
DEVIL'S ARMY

THE
DOOMSDAY
TRILOGY

BOOK 1

A GOLD EAGLE BOOK FROM
WORLDWIDE®

TORONTO • NEW YORK • LONDON
AMSTERDAM • PARIS • SYDNEY • HAMBURG
STOCKHOLM • ATHENS • TOKYO • MILAN
MADRID • WARSAW • BUDAPEST • AUCKLAND

First edition July 2002
ISBN 0-373-64284-9

Special thanks and acknowledgment to
Dan Schmidt for his contribution to this work.

DEVIL'S ARMY

Printed in U.S.A.

There and then our best men were killed.
                                        —Homer, *Odyssey*

Men must be judged by their words and deeds.
They pass sentence on themselves with their
actions. I provide justice.
                                        —Mack Bolan

THE
MACK BOLAN®
LEGEND

Nothing less than a war could have fashioned the destiny of the man called Mack Bolan. Bolan earned the Executioner title in the jungle hell of Vietnam.

But this soldier also wore another name—Sergeant Mercy. He was so tagged because of the compassion he showed to wounded comrades-in-arms and Vietnamese civilians.

Mack Bolan's second tour of duty ended prematurely when he was given emergency leave to return home and bury his family, victims of the Mob. Then he declared a one-man war against the Mafia.

He confronted the Families head-on from coast to coast, and soon a hope of victory began to appear. But Bolan had broken society's every rule. That same society started gunning for this elusive warrior—to no avail.

So Bolan was offered amnesty to work within the system against terrorism. This time, as an employee of Uncle Sam, Bolan became Colonel John Phoenix. With a command center at Stony Man Farm in Virginia, he and his new allies—Able Team and Phoenix Force—waged relentless war on a new adversary: the KGB.

But when his one true love, April Rose, died at the hands of the Soviet terror machine, Bolan severed all ties with Establishment authority.

Now, after a lengthy lone-wolf struggle and much soul-searching, the Executioner has agreed to enter an "arm's-length" alliance with his government once more, reserving the right to pursue personal missions in his Everlasting War.

1

It was his guaranteed ticket to Paradise. Assured of divine approval in the eyes of the God of his Koran, Hasab Shabak was to call the moment of truth on his own terms. The way God would want it. The coming onslaught would be not only for himself, but also to right a few of many atrocities inflicted on clan and country by the Great Satan.

There was no turning back from where he stood, packed in among the infidel cattle. Once he began sending as many of these godless savages to the fires of eternal damnation as possible, it wouldn't be long, perhaps the next stop, before he was forced to go out in a martyr's glory. Truth was, this decision was long overdue. The plan—details of which he wasn't privy to—was some dark conspiracy engineered by a North Korean.

Soon, within moments, the tool of the wrath of God was about to go to work, he thought, on this mass of devils entering Manhattan from their outer boroughs.

Just another day at the office, people? he thought, fighting back the laughter. Looking forward to that lunch at one of those gilded palaces, where the average American feasted like royalty? Oh, he'd seen that much, every day, in fact, while bussing plates off their tables, strangling down the rage over the sinful waste of food left for the garbage, baffled and seething still more by the injustice of how a single gluttonous American could spend more on a meal or a bottle of wine than the average Iraqi, who earned no more than three dollars a month.

Well, one car on the F train, at best, would soon prove a rolling coffin. Revenge was the day's special, and Shabak intended to serve it up cold. Indeed, it would be a day, he knew, long after his martyrdom and ascent to heaven, where the children and the grandchildren of the dead would remember what happened. Of course, the survivors would wail and gnash their teeth, never understand, much less seek out redemption on behalf of the sins of their fathers and their mothers.

No matter. No mercy, no exemptions.

To the smallest child on board, they were little more than fattened calves in his eyes, long since ready for slaughter. He could be sure, given what he'd seen in America so far, that down to lowliest infidel they all wallowed, smug and certain, from cradle to grave inside the honey-lined cocoons of money, food and pleasure. They looked oblivious, soft from wealth and privilege, no doubt, as he searched their faces for signs of life or even passing interest in his presence. Why was he surprised? Before stepping into the car, he had expected to find no less than human leeches who bloated themselves on the blood, sweat and suffering of peoples around the world they would never meet, much less care existed, as long as they were out of sight, out of mind, the poverty and misery of others little more than a sound bite from their nightly newscasts. Bearing in mind he had heard somewhere that most Americans couldn't even pick out their own state on a map, he decided their ignorance would become his bliss.

Deeper than contempt burned a feeling of superiority, of divine righteousness, as he continued scouring the faces buried in newspapers or paperbacks or pretending to stare at nothing while avoiding eye contact with their fellow passengers.

Unaware they were marked for extinction.

It was a shame, he concluded, he was only one warrior, two weapons, with an equal number of grenades. So many devils to slay, so few bullets.

It would have to do.

A part of him had another regret, as he ran a roving eye up and down the car, looking for any threat in the form of a policeman. They were known to frequent the subway, since America, the Korean had told him during one of many briefings, was a land of criminals.

Yes, he knew he was jumping the gun, so to speak, in danger of perhaps bringing an abrupt and violent end to the plans of his benefactors. Not to mention striking out on his own would bring a certain death sentence down on his head, as well as on his brother's transplanted family in Brooklyn. The innocent blood of Saddam Shabak's clan would be on his hands, but in the end, he decided life would be far better for the children in the next world. They ran the risk, after all, of forgetting their Islamic roots, forsaking their holy commitment to God and the Koran, as they grew up in this land where they only worshiped at the altar of money and sex. Yes, he thought, this was a subhuman culture, godless and without redemption, able to reach out any and everywhere to corrupt even the most innocent and purest of souls. Surely those people were an abomination in the eyes of God, soulless beasts who would corrupt and consume unless they were stopped.

He glanced at the woman in the short skirt, the whore baring long legs, crossed and sheathed in white hose, her perfume filling the air. The heated tug he felt in his crotch warned him she would have to be one of the first. Their women, he wondered, were they like that all over the land, showing off bodies in public, seeking to entice any man who came along? He suddenly recalled his amazement and confusion the first time he had seen one of the American talk shows. American women were allowed to voice opinions on their television, would even bully and shout down the men if they were disagreed with. Unheard of, he knew, in the Koran, where woman was created from the rib of Adam, meant by God to be a faithful, obedient and loving mate. What sort of men were these Americans? Sitting by, allowing brazen and shameless daughters and wives to flaunt their immorality in public forums. They had laws that even allowed for the legal killing of the unborn or permitted men to marry men. Indeed, he decided, being the indirect hand, responsible for the executions of his brother's children...well, death would spare their souls, save them from damnation.

And Shabak didn't think he could wait much longer to free himself of this cursed land. Surely Satan was alive and well in America. His own charade had gone on long enough.

As a former officer in the Iraqi army, a tank commander, no less, it had been a daily insult—despite the elaborate smoke screen to infiltrate him and the others into America—to bus tables, wash dishes while waiting for the phone to ring to call him to glory. Nearly a year now, he had endured masquerading as little more than an underpaid, overworked slave, held in thinly veiled contempt by the very people he intended to eventually kill.

No more.

Instead of allowing their mysterious Korean benefactor to determine his fate, Shabak, as a holy Islamic warrior, believed it was his right, his sacred duty to God, to chart his own path, choose the time and place where he would slay his enemies before pulling the pin and riding the big blast straight to heaven.

Actually, he thought, his fate had been carved in stone many years ago, before he'd even set foot in this land of fat bellies and fat wallets. The cowardly bombing of Baghdad by the western vultures, with their smart bombs, their laser-guided death delivered from a great distance assuring them of safety.

Well, they had no one but themselves to thank for the coming slaughter.

Shabak was surprised at how calm he felt. This was no dry run, no walk-through of some target on the horizon to blow up. Surprised next, yes, that the raw hatred he had come to accept like a second skin had receded behind the cold armor of vengeance when he made this final choice.

Besides, other than revenge, he had nothing left to live for. His two sons and his daughter were in Paradise, having been crushed beneath the rubble of the hospital where they had sought shelter from the American vultures during the war. Somehow his wife had survived, only life after the bombing had left her damaged worse than if she'd simply lost a leg or an arm. The shell of the woman who remained could not have been God's will, as Shabak briefly recalled the catatonic creature he'd come home to after the Americans had released him from one of their POW camps. For hours on end, he would watch the lifeless woman, praying as she stared at nothing. Sometimes she would mutter words he couldn't understand, or rock herself, rolling her head from side to side. Unable or unwilling to speak—much less rebuild their lives or bear him another child—she would erupt on occasion in hysterical outbursts that bordered on demonic whenever he attempted to reach out and hold her. In time, seeing that the woman he once knew and loved was dead and gone from him forever, he considered killing her, if nothing else than to put her out of her misery, send her to heaven where she could rejoin their children. But that had seemed too cruel, a sin against his own he didn't think he could live with, so he clung to hope that someday she would—

"Sir, are you all right?"

The American was staring at him, his cologne overpowering in Shabak's nose. He couldn't be certain if he'd cursed, but knew he needed to pull it back together before someone became suspicious. He muttered something at the American, looked away, feeling the train slowing for its next stop.

Shabak kept his hands buried deep in the pockets of his trench coat, his arm shielding the bulk of the compact M-12 Italian submachine gun, hand wrapped around the Heckler & Koch USP .45-caliber pistol. He was weighted down with four spare clips each for the instruments of his judgment. He twisted his body away from any passing contact as they disgorged onto the platform. He was ready, but wondered why he was hesitating. Was he afraid he was about to lose the desire to go through with it, believing instead his benefactors had something far bigger and more glorious in store?

No.

Despite himself, he started remembering the North Korean's words about the odd assemblage of weaponry. The benefactor—known only to him and his brothers-in-jihad during the briefings as the colonel—always appeared to be smiling. He never shared his private joke, but kept it to himself, as if mere Iraqi cannon fodder were too lowly or too stupid to understand whatever words of wisdom were on the tip of his tongue. Even still, the smiling Korean could never resist doling out the personal insights or schooling on how to proceed.

"You have been trained in the use of many weapons," the Korean had told them. "Do not come to prefer any one weapon. You see, once you have finished your mission and are on your way to your Paradise, the American authorities will be confused about the mix of weapons. Some Russian, some European, some Chinese, even some American. Confusion as to the origin of the supplier, you understand. Their American commando murderers do the same when they invade foreign countries, not wishing to leave behind evidence as to their true identities. They, like you, know their own deaths are simply part of the scheme.

"Now, once you begin the deed, you must spare no

one. Not even a child or a mother. No mercy, but I can see you understand this much. However, perhaps you will encounter one of their men who has seen one too many Jackie Chan movies. What I am telling you is do not underestimate the sudden impulse by one of their men to prove himself a hero."

"Excuse me," a man said, interrupting his memories.

There were two men. Shabak had moved a step or so toward the door, anticipating blocking off at least one exit, grateful there was some elbow room to get it jump-started. There were fairly unobstructed fields of fire for both ends of the aisle. The men were shouldering their way past him, bumping their way on through other passengers, men in suits clearing a path, heads bowed, eyes averted. For a moment, he found their hostility and rudeness most curious. He watched them glaring back, the coldness inside revived now, his grip tightening around the new American law-enforcement pistol. They had some sort of colored rags on their heads, with pant legs dragging the floor, the seats hanging down their rears to a near obscene point. Gangsters, or so they were called in America, he believed.

The Korean's voice came back. "You will see them in America, mostly in the cities. They call themselves disenfranchised, claim they are the voiceless underprivileged, forever crying that the majority rule has forced them to turn to crime. You will wonder about the sanity of this country, where their young carry weapons and sell poison to their own while casting the blame on someone else, where these young animals will shoot someone dead over the smallest insult or a simple look or for a pair of tennis shoes. Do not speak to them, do not stare at them and, by all means," the Korean had added with a chuckle, "do not wear expensive tennis shoes.

"Now, you may become confused by the mindless rage, the gratuitous vulgarity of their criminal class—contact with them will be unavoidable in the city—where you can plainly see no rhyme or reason for such atrocious behavior in a land that has more wealth, privilege and opportunity for all than any other nation on the planet, or in the whole of mankind's history for that matter. Except for my own country—and, of course, your nation, which, we all know, is rich in culture and things of honor. You may find yourself wishing to retaliate on the spot, strike them down for their impertinence and lack of manners. Resist the urge to kill needlessly and wait for your appointed hour."

"What you lookin' at?"

Shabak knew he was staring at the first two dead infidels. He only wished he could see himself in a mirror, as he felt an enigmatic smile shape his mouth that would have made the Korean proud. Several suits buried their faces deeper in newspapers, one or two of them slinking deeper into the car. Clearly, he thought, no heroes were going to be found here.

They were throwing each other looks, he saw, deciding what to do next, but shuffling toward him, just the same, as if the one was bolstered by the other's anger and hostility.

"I have many problems," Shabak told them. "Two of which I can see are to be solved right about now."

They pulled up short, uncertain, glancing at each other, grumbling curses.

Shabak was momentarily amazed at what Americans would tolerate, as he sensed he was one hundred percent on his own with these two, no one even glancing their way. "As for what I am looking at—I am looking at nothing. Absolutely nothing."

Shabak believed he could almost see their minds working, confusion gone next as the insult got them launched ahead, all rage and streaming curses. Shabak let the smile go, his limbs suddenly feeling lighter than air as he hauled out the pistol and shot them both high in the face, exit holes scalping the bandanas off their heads. One of them had appeared to be reaching inside his jacket, perhaps going for a knife, maybe a gun.

Shabak would never know, nor did he care, not giving them another thought as they dropped.

It was just the beginning.

The anticipated screaming hit the air next, figures bouncing off each other near the end of the car, diving beneath their seats or scrambling, shoving their way down the aisle for an exit. Maybe a dozen passengers closest to him remained seated, looking to him like frozen puppets waiting only for him to jerk the strings. He suspected they were glued to their seats out of both fear and a hope that maybe the gangsters had simply pushed their luck with the wrong New Yorker, wrong place, wrong time when some city-dwelling vigilante decided enough was enough.

Shabak dispelled any notions they were safe when he dumped the handgun into his pocket and swung the compact subgun out in full view on its swivel rig.

Now with the adrenaline kicked in all the way, the moment seemed to carry him forward all by itself. He couldn't recall a time when he'd ever felt this alive, whole, in charge. He savored the moment of their terror, the car rolling on, all of them knowing full well they were trapped and destined now to be slaughtered. They were fuzzy shapes in his sight, their shouts of panic coming to him from some great distance beyond the roar in his ears. He was vaguely aware of the sound of his own voice, bellowing out insults and cursing them in Arabic as he held back on the subgun's trigger. Number-three victim was a suit dropping his paper, streaked with blood and dribbling brain matter from one of the gangsters. The man held up pinkish hands and begged for his life, something about how he had a wife and sons.

So did I, Shabak thought, once upon a time.

Firing on, Shabak laughed as the paper vanished in a cloud of shreds and red mist. Swinging his aim, Shabak spotted the whore next, rushing to join the stampede surging for the back of the car, as if she could save herself in a crowd. He chopped her down with a burst up the back, flinging her into the rolling mass, deadweight bowling down a few screamers in flight.

It was reflex and a sort of angry, giddy will from there on, wheeling around, aiming the muzzle at anything that sat or tried to hunch for cover or run. He found no heroes daring to make some suicide charge, so two full clips later he was walking over mounds of bodies, silencing the pleas from a few hiders under the seats with short bursts on the slow roll. A whimpering noise, and he turned, found a woman huddling two small boys to her bosom. They didn't look American, and he thought she was pleading for the lives of her sons in Farsi.

He stepped up and told the woman, "It is Allah's

will. They—and you—will be better off in the next world."

Six or seven rounds later, he finished sending them on to Paradise, mother sliding off the seat to drape crimson ruins over her children. Then he spotted the cop, the uniformed figure throwing open the rear door to the car, pistol in hand.

Shabak palmed a fragmentation grenade. The policeman was nearly through the doorway and barking for the passengers to get down when the Iraqi armed the steel bomb and let it fly. The subgun chattering next, he drove the policeman to cover behind the door with a flurry of 9 mm rounds that rattled off the frame, the survivors crying out, huddled on top of each other when ricochets rounds snapped the air, scored flesh from the tangled pile.

As the grenade blew, the air filled with shrieking and howls of pain for a moment, lost quickly to the stammering of his subgun. He marched on, the smells of cordite, emptied bowels and blood swelling his senses, a heady intoxicant, it seemed, that fueled him to new heights of fury and determination. He was pleased the subgun had little recoil, didn't tend to rise up as most SMGs did, allowing him four to five quick kills with not much effort or aim. The third 40-round clip home and bolt racked, he surveyed the carnage, homed in on moaners. There were a few still clinging to hope, calling out for mercy, help, whatever.

And Shabak singled them out and gave perhaps seven or eight more devils a quick burst to the face, relishing the taste of their blood on his lips as gory juices struck him in the face, their screams for mercy ringing in his ears. Briefly he found himself both amazed and appalled at how terrified these Americans were of dying, unwilling to leave behind, he guessed, their worlds of money and pleasure. He had heard how they had watched the bombing of Baghdad on their televisions, twenty-four-hour coverage, in fact, as Iraqi bridges, buildings and hospitals were pounded to rubble, crushing to death scores of women and children. Perhaps a few of them in that very car, he suspected, had even viewed the destruction of his country while gorging themselves on food and drink, chortling to each other that the Iraqis were simply getting what they deserved.

Fair enough, he decided, the tables, as he believed they would say, were now turned.

At the far end of the car, he noted the door, smoking and warped, bodies and body parts strewed in front of the roiling cloud. No more of New York's finest. In the other direction he found more mass panic, as passengers in the next car were bumping and grinding their way to gain distance from the slaughter. Shabak was walking on top of bodies now, the subgun's muzzle sweeping around as he searched between the seats for live ones, when he noticed the train had stopped. It was difficult to see through the windows, where long smears of blood or brain matter ran in jagged streams like obscene graffiti, all but obscuring any decent surveillance of the tunnel.

He heard them crying out in the next cars. He wondered if they were fleeing the train, but that wasn't possible unless the driver also opened the doors on his car. Or was it? How long had it been since he'd begun the massacre? He thought he saw shadows passing beneath the running curtains of blood. He moved to the middle of the car, swiveling his search from one door to the other. The police, he knew, or SWAT or some rapid-response team would be on the way. Or were they already boarding the train, running at the car of death from both directions?

It was impossible to take an accurate body count, but Shabak had to figure he had tallied something in the neighborhood of fifty to sixty kills. Not great, but good enough to see him soaring past the gates and into Paradise. The last decision was made next. Waiting for the American authorities to storm the car, Shabak knelt in a puddle of his enemies' blood, believed he was facing toward Mecca. He tried to tune his ears into the sounds of feet stomping his direction, ready for them to show up, but he focused on one last round of prayers. He prayed for the souls of his late family. He prayed for his brother and for the souls of his brother's family, soon to be slain by their benefactors for his personal jihad. He prayed that when he saw them in Paradise they would understand what he had done and why, and forgive him this impulsive transgression against them.

He heard them coming now, surprised for a moment how quickly they had responded. Slipping his hand into his coat pocket, he fumbled with the grenade, finally got the pin pulled, felt the spoon drop. They were barreling through both doors now, shouting for him to get his hands up. Shabak rose and bulled ahead into the wall of bullets fired from the policemen unfortunate enough to be the first into the car.

IT WAS THE WORST and the last day of his life. The grief was wound tight, dammed up in Saddam Shabak's chest, holding back for the moment, but it was set to blow, come gushing out of his mouth in a wailing that, once begun, would never end...until he took his own life or was shot dead by the visitors he knew were on the way.

"This reporter cannot even begin to describe the horror..."

He'd heard the initial reports already, the phone call not more than twenty minutes after the first special broadcast. He hit the mute button on the remote, no longer requiring the loud volume to mask their cries, the sound of dead bodies crashing to the kitchen floor. It was done, and he didn't care if some neighbor called in a domestic disturbance to the police or not.

His own brother had already bulled ahead, striking out for his own personal jihad before the appointed time. So what did it matter if he was left behind now to go to Paradise in some shoot-out with the authorities in his own apartment? Still, how could Hasab have been so willful and reckless, knowing before he fired the first bullet that his actions would have consequences beyond his own death? It was extremely selfish.

He felt so numb, stained by what he'd done, he believed even a prayer to God for mercy and understanding seemed like a grievous blasphemy that might only reserve for him a special place of fire and agony in the bowels of Hell if he uttered aloud the first plea for forgiveness. He dropped onto the couch, buried his face in a hand, sucking down his grief. He didn't need the voice of the Korean over the phone, the newscast about the subway massacre or the missing weapons in the cache hidden beneath the floorboard in the hall closet to tell him what had happened, who was responsible or what was coming. His life was numbered in minutes.

He looked at the pistol, still clutched and smoking in his hand, wondered what life would have been like if only he had stayed in Iraq. But, no, he was Saddam— which meant "the Stubborn One." And he had made the choice, freely and with righteous anger to burn following the war, intending to find a way to strike back against the enemies of all Iraqi peoples, whatever it took, whoever could help. Even though his own immediate family had somehow been spared the horror of the war, either by an act of God or some fluke of fate, he still carried his hatred, a badge of honor in his eyes, for the Americans ever since. He moved chemical and biological ordnance around the country, whisking it from under the very noses of the CIA and their inspectors, in fact. He also did strong-arm work, killing Kurds, too. Then he was called upon to go and fulfill a destiny that had only once seemed an impossible dream.

Now his quest for vengeance, so close at hand, would never see its holy fruition.

It had been quick, for the most part, beyond Jahih's begging for him not to do it, a moment's hesitation before he put one bullet each in the heads of his wife and three sons. He would never have thought this moment would come to pass in his worst nightmare. But hadn't he, his brother and the others been warned during the briefings this was exactly the sort of horror they could expect?

The North Korean colonel's voice seemed to intrude into his thoughts as he sat, staring at nothing, hating himself for what he had done—what his brother had done. "Should there be any breach in security for any reason, should any one of you be found out, far worse still, should one of you be captured by the Americans, then a phone call will be placed to your residence. If there is no man present, should he be in the custody of the Americans, then two men assigned by myself for this unfortunate task will come to visit your families. I do not think I have to spell out what will happen to your families in that event."

Having already gone ahead and spared himself the shame of watching a stranger execute his family, Shabak rose to follow through with the next step of covering up any trail that would point toward his country of birth or raise suspicions on the part of the American FBI. Perhaps the plan, whatever it was, would succeed without him. At least he could hope the blood on his hands would be avenged in due course.

He went and removed the passports from the top desk drawer, the most painful act coming next when he gathered any photographs he'd kept of his family. He dumped it all into a metal wastebasket, lit a cigarette then doused any evidence in the apartment of their existence, real or false, with lighter fluid. He removed the batteries from the smoke alarm, then torched his own passport, the face and assumed identity of Ali Hassham of Lebanon melting before his eyes.

He was back on the couch when the expected knock on the door came. He had left it open, as per the instructions from the voice on the phone. Two short, slender Korean men in dark suit jackets stepped into the living room. One of them toted a large duffel bag, while the other shut the door. Shabak turned away from them, detecting the look of disapproval, even judgment in their eyes. The first man went to the hall closet where he began stuffing the bag with the few pistols, grenades and the single remaining subgun. They knew where to go, of course, since Shabak was aware this apartment was set up by their North Korean sponsors specifically as his waiting place, the weapons already hidden away before he even set foot on American soil.

Shabak drew on his cigarette, found his hand shaking. He wondered if he was trembling with shame or outrage that the North Korean was already threading the sound suppressor on his pistol, moving into the kitchen as if checking to make certain he hadn't left any of his family alive by accident. Shabak felt his anger rising at the mental picture of the man toeing his family with his shoes or feeling for heartbeats that weren't there.

He finished his cigarette, grinding it out by foot on the floor. He could feel the North Korean moving up behind him.

"It would be better if you did it yourself."

Shabak chuckled. It wasn't difficult to interpret the point between the lines. Family man goes berserk, slays wife and children, shoots himself. No motive, no reason, happens all the time. America. A stressful, dangerous place to live, where most murders occur between family members. Not even the police would be baffled or pursue an investigation. At least that was how the colonel had explained it.

"May I have a moment to pray?"

"There is no time for such nonsense."

Perhaps it was his overpowering guilt and shame.

Perhaps it was being denied his last request or perhaps it was his potential executioner's choice of words and tone. Maybe it was a combination that made Saddam Shabak snap inside, grabbing up the pistol, lurching to his feet, turning the weapon on the insolent bastard.

But he never got the chance to fire.

2

It was something of a rare occasion when Mack Bolan found Hal Brognola out for an apparent stroll. A workaholic, the big Fed usually earned his room and board in the name of national security in one of two places—either in his office at the Justice Department or at Stony Man Farm out in the Shenandoah Valley of Virginia, where America's number-one ultracovert operation was housed. Bolan, who was also known as the Executioner, was at the Farm when he got the call from Brognola to saddle up—weapons and gear ready—and chopper in to Reagan National where his longtime friend had a driver standing by.

The soldier now read the worried expression on Brognola's face as he strode deeper across the manicured expanse of lawn. It was the time of day where the happy-hour bunch was winding it down from the Hill to Georgetown, waiting for the herds of nine-to-five commuters to thin out. As for Bolan's friend, there was rarely the time or privilege in his world for a few quickies at the local pub to rub elbows, schmooze over the day's doings. The big Fed's rank and classified job de-

scription also saw him pulling double duty as Stony
Man liaison to the President of the United States, who
sanctioned missions for the Farm's warriors. The Justice Man's time clock was never punched, but it was real
simple—twenty-four hours, seven days a week. Thus,
it was no stretch for the soldier to conclude this was no
walk in the park for Brognola, or rather the Mall in this
case.

Duty beckoned, he suspected, and Bolan was there
to get the particulars before moving on for a new campaign. The Executioner put on his game face.

The soldier angled toward the big Fed, who saw him
coming, strode next for an unoccupied bench and parked
himself. Despite a nip to the air, Bolan found the jog-
gers, cyclists and scattered gaggles of meandering
tourists still out en force. Normally the director of the
Sensitive Operations Group didn't conduct business out
in the open, where passing ears might pick up matters
pertaining to national security.

Closing on Brognola, Bolan read his friend's own
game face. On second study, Bolan detected some wistful but weary observing of the various historic landmarks staggered from east to west. The Capitol
Building. The white granite monolith of the National Air
and Space Museum. The red castle marking the Smith-
sonian. The Washington Monument. Bolan sensed his
friend's mood of solemn reverie and took in the sights
himself. He could well appreciate the need to get out
once in a while, stretch the legs or sit idle, even when
duty beckoned. It wasn't so much the need to grab some
fresh air, but maybe the warrior psyche simply had to

review, assess and digest somehow all the hard miles logged in defense of what the landmarks stood for.

Freedom.

It was something neither man ever took for granted. And sometimes, Bolan knew, what was taken for granted could be gone tomorrow, snatched away, or trampled by the savages, unless a man understood in the core of his being what it was he had. And was likewise willing to go the extra mile to insure truth, justice and liberty for one and for all.

Bolan took a seat next to his friend. "So, what's up?"

Brognola smiled. "I gave it a few hours, fielding the usual calls, picking the brains of reliable sources before I sounded any alarms your way."

"Referring to the situation in New York."

"Right. Feelers out, called in a few markers to get the scuttlebutt."

"You're going to tell me what happened wasn't just the random act of some disgruntled New Yorker who was mugged one too many times."

Brognola gnawed on his unlit cigar. "If what I suspect pans out in even the slimmest, most remote way, shape or form, this is way beyond one lunatic who thinks death-wish-type vigilantism should be the eleventh commandment. Okay, first a little background, straight from my sources, with more than a fair share of digging and detective work from my own people at Justice and the FBI. Bear with me on some of the obvious.

"We both know the last two Administrations tried and failed to bomb Iraq back into the Stone Age. Not necessarily through any fault on their behalf, it's just that their leader is that one mosquito in the room you can never catch with a swatter. We know the CIA failed— miserably—to try and take him down using his own people, all of whom were wasted during any one of a dozen attempted coups against the great mustache since the end of the Gulf War."

"Right, as usual. So far, so bad."

"You know about the genocide campaign against the Kurds in the north and, of course, the CIA-UN weapons inspectors were long since sent packing. In the proverbial nutshell, it's all left him with plenty of elbow room to carry on putting together the mother of all bombs, keep on gassing Kurds, execute relatives, rattle his saber over the coffee, muffins and the head of whatever son-in-law or ranking officer fell out of his graces that day."

"On goes the party."

Brognola grunted. "We still fly sorties, of course, drop a few dozen tons of ordnance on his head some days when he's in an especially pissy mood."

"Business as usual over in Mesopotamia."

"Or it's business in the unusual. Okay, so the leader is still up there, head of the class of Uncle Sam's Bad Boys Club, and our side would like nothing more than to take him out. But between his multiple palaces, his four-hundred-foot yacht, where he uses a human shield of foreign dignitaries while tooling around the Tigris, tack on God only knows how many underground labyrinths where he buries himself when he hears what he calls 'the hostile crows' coming to say hello...well, it's little wonder he's still Mr. Fun of the Islamic fundamentalist party."

Brognola paused as an elderly lady with a small dog

walked past. Riding out the wait, Bolan knew the big Fed was leading up to the clincher. Brognola was not one to waste time on frivolous sound bites. "Ma'am," Brognola said, shooting her something of a patronizing smile, then nodding at the lady, who steered the dog well clear of the bench.

"At any rate, Iraq has recently become open to air traffic from all points. Baghdad's not exactly up there on my choice spot for a vacation, but you've got Jordan and Egypt, allegedly allies to Uncle Sam, leading the parade for the rest of the Arab world who wants their leader and Iraq brought back into the cozy bosom of civilization. Lift sanctions, no strings, let the oil flow, the war's over, what's the problem."

"Let it be, in other words."

"Yeah. No hard feelings, we should adopt a kinder, gentler approach to him and his butchers. They've suffered enough. So lately, instead of trying to shove a thousand-pound bomb up his nose, and risk blowing some Egyptian delegation back across the Sinai, our side has taken to parking satellites over ancient Babylon. Monitoring the air traffic, sifting through the cast of characters turning up on satellite imagery, stuff like that."

"Telling me we've picked up a rogue's gallery, doing more than just sharing the champagne with him on his yacht."

"Try North Koreans on for size. Try an esteemed entourage of officers and what we believe are special-forces goons from above the thirty-eighth parallel, there in what the CIA and the NSA believe is a military advisory capacity."

"Nice to know our intelligence folks still know how to sugarcoat and spin."

"Well, I defy them to sugarcoat one Kim Jong Il, son of the late Kim Il Sung, seen yukking it up with Iraq's leader and some lady friends. You've heard of Dr. Germ?"

"She's the leading lady in chemical death, the brains behind his chemical-weapons program. Earned her Ph.D. in plant toxins at the University of East Anglia, her education funded, I believe, by the British government."

"I'll never accuse you of idling away your free time catching up on soaps," Brognola cracked. "Back to the good doctor. The Britons are still wiping the omelette off their faces over where and how she acquired her higher learning and to what end. The CIA is also ducking the occasional hand grenade lobbed their way by politicos in the know on that score. For years they knew her talents were being tested on Iraqi prisoners, Kurds, any and all Iranian POWs unfortunate enough to get scooped up on the wrong side of the border during their leader's eight-year attempt to become the Iraqi version of Patton. Part of the problem now is we no longer have eyes and ears in the country."

"Courtesy of Langley."

"You got it. Not only did they fumble the ball on more than one occasion, but the CIA bailed out on their operatives in Iraq when UNSCOM packed it in."

"Left them twisting in the noose."

"Literally. Any ops they want to tell the numbers crunchers on the Hill they still have under contract over there to watch him have long since been digested by the buzzards. Now we discover, just for one thing, Kim and Dr. Germ aren't bashful about the photo ops for our eyes in the sky."

"I hear exchange program."

"No tea leaves, crystal balls or Tim Russert with his board to tell both of us what the future holds if two of the most dangerous and volatile countries in the world decide to go further than singing 'Kumbaya' together."

"No secret where Iraq stands."

"Missile technology. They still have plenty of missiles lying around. Their leader even has a couple of nukes ready to fly, but they lack the fissile core."

"We hope."

"Plus he's in desperate shape as far as getting the required and all-divine guidance systems—we hope."

"Enter North Korea."

"Smart money says we're looking at some end game in the brewing stages."

"But no bottom line?"

"Not yet."

"How does the subway massacre play into all this?"

"I'm almost there. Okay, we've got North Korean 'advisers' apparently arming and training Iraqis. We've got Kim and Dr. Germ exchanging goo-goo eyes. Now, say what you will about Kim Jong—despot, psychopath, pathological liar with delusions of grandeur—"

"You mean he didn't discover all those scientific theories? Or create the car and the toaster—and the Internet—like the Democratic People's Republic of Korea claims he did?"

Brognola returned Bolan's wry grin. "Nor has he walked on the moon, written a thousand epic novels in one year or invented the wheel like the good old DPRK tell the starving masses north of the thirty-eighth parallel. Hey, you still wear the jaded wit pretty well for a guy who's been sitting on the sidelines for a couple days."

"You know what they say about idle hands." Bolan lost the look, his eyes turning hard. "Kim Jong's a butcher, no more, no less."

"I hear that loud and clear. This guy sits around all day, according to our intel, spends a million bucks a year on Hennessy, watches *Rambo* and *Star Trek* reruns...it's hard to believe this buffoon, a fat, alcoholic scam artist who—besides thinking our own State Department can somehow land him his own talk show on cable—is the mastermind behind a number of terrorist attacks. The same guy who tried to whack the South Korean president in Burma, excuse me, Myanmar."

"The very same lunatic who plotted and brought down that Korean Air jetliner back in '87. Sometimes it's the clowns who can fool even the discerning eye the most. By the time you see past the smile or the tears, it's usually too late in the game."

"If he's trying to smile and bullshit his way down the Tigris with Iraq's leader, it looks like the Iraqi has bitten."

"And beyond this latest gathering of a psycho circus?"

"Two items. One—our martyr on the F train. Took himself out with a grenade as he charged the guns of the first New York cops on the scene."

"I heard."

Rage danced through Brognola's eyes. "This asshole

murdered fifty-plus commuters, Striker, most of them
where they sat. I'm talking mothers with kids, too. The
body count is still going up as they try to figure out
which arms and legs belong to which torsos and so on.
And five cops dead, two on the critical list."

Bolan felt his own fury rising.

And then Brognola dropped the bomb. "The FBI believes they tracked down where the bastard lived.
Brooklyn apartment, Atlantic Avenue, heavy with the
Mideast crowd. Seems a concerned citizen called in a
domestic disturbance. The police responded to the
apartment in question. They found what at first appeared
a murder-suicide, a family man who went berserk, recent immigrant, executed his wife and children, then
took his own life. That was the running scenario until
the FBI took over. The gentlemen in question might
have had a hard time shooting himself right between the
eyes, then putting another round through his heart, then
making the weapon vanish with him on his way to the
great beyond. And the waters grow murkier next when
I tell you the concerned citizen was questioned, just
happened to see two gentlemen of Asian origin coming
from the apartment."

"Of course, no weapons found, no ID."

"The Feds found a wastebasket full of what they believe
were documents, passports, the works, burned to crisp."

"And we're thinking our lunatic on the F train got
ahead of the program."

"And that just maybe he was shipped here from Iraq.
And the mysterious Asian gents—North Koreans, I'd
wager—were marched in by the sponsors to tie up a
loose end before the Feds came knocking."

"Could be the start of an elimination game."

"My thinking exactly. A whole cell of Iraqi lunatics, ready to shoot and blow up half of New York. Only now one of their own has mucked up the play and the sponsors are sending in the cleanup boys."

"We're still reaching."

"Could be, but I don't think so. Here's something of a clincher. After they questioned the neighbors of the apartment, I'm hearing the description of the bastard on the F train by the police who survived the final blast matches that of an individual who shared the abattoir in question."

"So, you want me to go to New York."

"The Man," Brognola said, referring to the President, "wants you in New York, ASAP."

"What are the particulars on my end?"

"Attached, as commander and chief, to a special task force out of my office that specializes in hunting terrorists on U.S. soil. I'll have the blanks filled in on that score by the time I get back to the office."

And the soldier knew his friend would. By the time Brognola wrapped it up, the Executioner knew he was a short flight away from getting cut loose, carte blanche to do what must be done to uncover any loose Iraqi cannons about to run amok and slaughter any more innocent American citizens. As he thought about those slain commuters, he caught the look in Brognola's eyes. It told him the big Fed damn near pitied anybody who had helped that particular savage get safe and free passage to American soil. Almost, but actually far from it. Sometimes, they both knew, vengeance was simply part and parcel of a warrior's duty.

His heart beating a little faster, the Executioner felt his game face harden up a little more. He was good to go.

"DAD, DON'T YOU ever quit trying to save us from nuclear war?" Sara Shaw asked.

"A defensive shield over the earth, my dear, specifically the continental U.S., would prevent the other side's missiles from landing and turning our country into a radioactive wasteland that only the cockroach would inherit."

"Thermonuclear bombs lighting up the heavens, you mean. What about the fallout? What if one of a dozen or so ICBMs somehow gets through your magic laser net? One would be more than enough to start World War III."

"I'm working on that particular problem now," Thomas Shaw answered.

"It's not too often you get both your daughters in the same place at the same time. Can you give it a rest?"

"I'll consider shutting it down, at least in the interests of quality family time, the day you quit smoking."

"And bring home Mr. Right, too?"

"Trust me, I'll decide if he's right or not. I'm reserving that one and only privilege I'm asking as a father to his twenty-something daughter."

"Four. Twenty-four, Dad."

"Yes. My big girl, all grown up."

Sara took a seat at her father's workstation. He was smiling when he said that, but she often wondered if she had somehow let him down, searching the eyes behind his glasses for a moment before he turned his full attention back to the computer's monitor. She couldn't think how she might have disappointed him, other than not putting her journalism degree to work for her as soon as she graduated college, maybe land that steady job at the *Washington Post,* giving her the advice, hinting the future was now. Cub reporter on the climb up the ladder of success, indeed, the present stable and secure, future nothing but roses, dad proud.

Instead, she postponed the future, whatever might lie ahead, opting to bartend to make ends meet, a trip once a year to Europe or Miami Beach when her Annandale apartment started feeling too small and she grew too restless. Well, at least she hadn't gotten pregnant, didn't do drugs and she'd never fallen into a promiscuous lifestyle during her college years or since, as a number of her girlfriends had. She smoked cigarettes, her only vice, liked to go out with her friends once in a while, maintaining her right to independence, Cosmo girl.

On the other hand her father, she knew, was old school, fashioned decades ago by Catholic tradition to believe in a world where there was no gray. Perhaps that was the problem, she thought. The world had changed, but Thomas Shaw still believed it was the fifties, when birth control meant the rhythm method. She suspected he didn't much care for the attitudes of modern American females, although he was a perfect gentleman, married to her mother for something close to forty years. He didn't curse, drink or smoke. He was moderate in everything he did, beyond, of course, his work. She often wondered what it was he did to unwind, or if there was some secret eccentricity he reserved for himself.

Oh, well, part of growing up, she believed, was simply accepting what couldn't be changed. Twice a year she might make the trip out to Middleburg to see her family when her younger sister was on break from college. Maybe it was enough that they were all gathered under the same roof. If she'd been younger, still getting whisked from school to school and state to state because of her father's position with the military branch of NASA or the NSA—and she was never certain whom he pledged allegiance to—she might have squawked some when old dad was too busy to pay her more than a passing interest.

His life was his work.

She watched as his fingers flew over the keyboard, computerized graphics of satellites, what she believed were grid maps, missiles in flight over the North Pole, and numbers in the corner scrolling through at light speed. She might find him remiss when it came to what he might see as mundane matters pertaining to simple hearth and home, but her father was an important man, his work top secret, or rather classified, she knew, in the jargon of his world. Had his work been "Eyes only," meaning the official badge of the Strategic Defense Initiative with Department of Defense at the bottom would be plastered at the top of the monitor...in that case she knew the grim bodyguard assigned to the house, Mr. Congeniality, as she referred to him, wouldn't have allowed her to set on foot into this sanctuary.

Over the years she had tried to understand what it was her father did. Sometimes she tried to engage him in conversation about Star Wars, but it was something of a rare solar eclipse when he discussed his work, which, of course, could leave her that much more curious. Space warfare, in layman terms, she thought, was pretty much the stuff of science fiction. He called what he was attempting to create—missiles that would knock enemy missiles out of the sky or hundreds of miles above the earth—like hitting a bullet with a bullet. It was all beyond her, but still she admired him, despite her ignorance on the subject. For one thing he was part of a group called the Titan Four, missile geniuses, two of which—her father included—had been interviewed on various cable talk shows. His world might be alien to her, but she still knew a celebrity when she saw one. She had taped the episodes for posterity, and to show him off for her friends if the mood struck her. So it was her father's task to develop both theoretical scenarios and create advanced blinding systems. She'd heard him talk briefly about laser-guided warheads on space stations, space sensors, a web of orbiting mirrors needed to tangle up any missiles launched out of the earth's atmosphere, to be shot down before they had a chance to reenter and vaporize American cities. Long-wavelength infrared probes, DEWs—or Directed Energy Weapons—exo- and endoatmospheric interceptors...it boggled her mind to even attempt to fathom how her father could keep it all straight in his head. But to her, despite what might be a strained relationship at times, he was brilliant.

"Mom's been slaving away on your favorite dish."

"Linguine and clams?"

"With red sauce."

"Slaving, you say?"

She frowned. "Bad choice of words."

"You're asking, then, how much longer?"

She was about to do just that when the intercom buzzed, the bodyguard's voice cutting through the study, all business and concern.

"It's all right, Rodgers. What I have up is not classified."

"Sir, but..."

"We can bend the rules this one time. Thank you for your concern."

"I guess he'll report you now to the principal?"

"Merely doing his job."

"Is it even necessary for him to be around?"

"Yes, it is, my dear. Unfortunately, there have been...some breaches, I understand, in security at two different installations, some rumors I have heard... threats."

"Threats? Against who? How come I don't like the sound of any of this, Dad?"

"Nothing for you to be alarmed about."

"You're not saying you or the rest of us are in any danger?"

"The world has changed, Sara."

If it wasn't for the seriousness of the talk, she would have smiled at this admission.

"You needn't look so surprised," he said, smiling. "Yes, even staid old dad can admit times have changed."

"So the guard stays, gun and all."

"For now."

"Until these security breaches are plugged up? Should I plan on buying him something for next Christmas? Cleaning oil, or whatever it is he uses to polish his gun?"

He was smiling now, but his silence told her she

wasn't going to get much more out of him on the subject of security, or his thoughts on any perceived or real threat to himself and the rest of the family. If she stopped and thought about it, she knew his work alone placed him in some shadow world where classified documents were stolen or sold all the time. The danger might be way out there on the fringes for her father, Rodgers with his gun always there to watch his back, but what was to stop foreign agents from putting an offer to him that he couldn't refuse? Her father's work was on the cutting edge, jealously guarded, but what if...?

She stopped herself before the train of paranoia could sour a mood that was on the verge of lapsing into full-blown annoyance anyway. This was Middleburg, after all. Horse country, big Thoroughbred money. Each home pretty much sat on pristine acres of wooded land, fortified enclaves where folks spent more on security than most Washingtonians made in one year. This was far removed from any spy central where armed guards patrolled and searched every nook and cranny for saboteurs, shadow assassins.

"I'm going see if Mom and Patti need any help," she said, but knew she'd cave to the urge for a smoke as soon as she was out of the room.

"Leave the window in the bathroom open. By the way, cigarettes are not biodegradeable when you flush them down the toilet."

"Thanks, Dad, I'll remember that."

She was grateful when she found Rodgers wasn't hovering around when she made her exit, veered next on a beeline for the guest room. It was on the bottom floor, close to the patio, so she had quick access for a late-night smoke if she wanted a change of scenery from the adjoining bathroom. She heard her mother clanging about in the kitchen, found her sister setting up the dinner table. She decided against some lame excuse for not assisting them, vanishing into the bathroom before someone noticed she was making herself scarce for a smoke break.

Closing the door, she lit up, then opened the window. She was blowing out the first stream of smoke, when she thought she heard the bleating of helicopter blades, coming from some point but growing closer from beyond the dark mass of rolling hills to the west. She was about to turn away from the window when the chopper landed on their property. There were no lights on the helicopter, but enough glow shone from the lampposts near the gazebo for her to make out—

She nearly dropped the cigarette on the carpet. They were shadows, running hard across the patio, moving like some well-oiled machine, but she made out the distinct shapes of machine guns in their hands.

She felt the panic and terror rise up in her throat, her mind racing for answers that eluded her. Or did they, the answer simply a shout away from her father's work study? Did this have something to do with the mysterious breach of security her father alluded to?

She heard the shouting beyond the closed door, the chaos of several voices rolling her way in various degrees of anger and confusion, fear and demands. Oh, God, she thought, what was happening? She thought she was going to be sick. Why hadn't the security alarm sounded, alerting them that invaders, armed to the teeth, had stormed their house? Realization of what was happening and why began to take shape in her mind as she searched for her voice. She was trapped, but she wouldn't allow herself to be at the mercy of strangers with guns, not if she intended to help her family. But how? She dumped the cigarette in the toilet to a splash and a sizzle, glanced out the window in time to see more shadows with guns barreling through the kitchen door, her mother and sister shrieking in panic. A voice was drifting her way, as someone bellowed for her to be found. Her father was out there, demanding to know what was happening, who they were.

Think quick. She knew what was happening, even as she tried to lie to herself that everything was going to be fine.

This was a kidnapping. And these men, whoever they were, were there to snatch her father. His work, through no fault of his own, was about to see them abducted, maybe worse. Taken where? For how long?

A part of her demanded she charge out into the living room, but she believed if she hid she could better serve her family. If she could somehow escape the coming search. And do what? The logical course of action, naturally, would be to phone the police, the FBI, whoever would come there.

She ran for the guest room, crawling under the bed when she caught the babble of voices speaking in some rapid-fire Asian language. Okay, the window was open, and when they hit the bathroom she could only hope and pray they believed she was outside, fleeing into the woods, running to get help. She could feel their menacing presence, scurrying about in the bathroom now, so close she feared they'd smell the smoke clinging to her body. Again they were talking in Asian until another voice barked, "Speak English!"

"She is gone!"

"She's not gone. She's outside somewhere. Get out there and find her! You have two minutes!"

Sara Shaw held her breath as she heard the bathroom door leading to the bedroom bang open. She could see the man's legs, some sort of combat boots, just feet away from her face. She hugged the floor, not trusting that her ploy had worked, the air locked in her chest, waiting him out.

Leave, she silently urged.

He left, after what felt like an hour. For a moment she detested her own relief and wondered if she was simply being a coward. Hiding, like some little child from the bogeyman, hoping she wasn't found. But what was she going to do against men with guns anyway? She heard one of them cursing from the bathroom, and knew she was safe from discovery as the sound of boots tromping over tile faded.

Knowing she was helpless, defenseless against this unknown menace, Sara offered up a silent prayer for the safety of her family. It was the only thing she could do until the invaders left and she could call the police.

THOMAS SHAW KNEW what was happening and why, even before he burst into the living room. The only questions left hanging were the identities of the invaders, and how they'd slipped past the security system. This was just the sort of moment he had dreaded for years, aware his work jeopardized the lives of his family. He never believed the day would come, but there he was, now witnessing his worst nightmare.

They were there for the work he had stored on disk, no question, all the classified data he had on the building and refinement of the guidance systems for the Medusa satellite. He would gladly give it to them, everything, if only they would leave his family unharmed. If he simply handed over his classified work on SDI, his superiors would eventually question his motives under their microscope. It would cost him more than just his security clearances, perhaps even his job.

He was forging ahead into what felt like an invisible wall of fear, when he spotted Rodgers pulling away from a group of four Asians who had his wife and daughter corralled on the couch and under the muzzles of automatic weapons. Now he knew, as he stared at Rodgers, how they had slipped the security net.

"Why?"

It was the only thing he could think of to ask a man he had trusted with his life and the lives of his family. The answer galled him, but he wasn't surprised.

"For the money. What else?"

He was calling out to his wife and daughter, worried why Sara wasn't in the living room, when a figure in black detached himself from a mix of Asians and Americans streaming out of the hallway that led to Sara's room. They hadn't found her, or if they had...

Before he could begin to try to comprehend the insanity of the moment, shout out a barrage of questions, a man with gray eyes, matching skin and white buzz cut strode up to Rodgers. The man fixed a sound suppressor to his pistol, then, without warning, shot Rodgers in the back of the head. Shaw froze at the sight of blood taking to the air, less than two feet away, his wife screaming now, loud enough, he feared, to send the neighbors running.

"And we appreciate the help. Now, Mr. Shaw..."

Cold-blooded murder, and this man acted as if it were nothing worse than simply flushing a toilet.

"Don't hurt my family. I'll give you anything you want."

"And so you shall. As for your family, sir, whether or not they stay breathing is up to you and to them."

Shaw was about to brush past the man when the pistol seem to frame itself in his face. "Stay put. Do as you're told and everything will work out."

"We can't find the other one."

Shaw felt the hope flickering back, aware Sara had escaped as one of the Asians gave the man in gray the report. It was dashed next by the realization this might simply enrage the leader into another impulse killing.

"It doesn't matter. We're out of here. We'll tie them up and blindfold them on the way."

"Where are you taking us?" Shaw heard his wife demand, the exchange nearly muted as his own roar of silent anger and terror filled his ears. "Thomas, give them what they want!"

"Oh, he will, ma'am, don't you worry. It just may take a little longer than you like. Could even take some persuasion that might get a little rough—or unsavory," the leader said, smiling at the women. "Sorry, folks, there's no time to pack your toothbrushes."

And Shaw knew this was only the beginning of being held captive. He read the cold look in the man's eyes for what it was. Doom, plain and simple—tomorrow, the day after or next week, but it would come.

Shaw well suspected what it was he was supposed to do, give up, create. And when he was finished, his purpose served, he knew they were all dead.

The last thing he remembered hearing, as he was grabbed and shoved ahead, was the leader ordering his study packed up for the ride.

3

Colonel Bok Chongjin of the North Korean special forces believed he understood Americans better than they understood themselves. It was the mentality, an appetite whetted by generations of greed, he thought, where the average American barbarian could easily be manipulated to his advantage, do his bidding, if the price was right. If, Chongjin decided, he played his cards correctly from there on—balancing the scales somewhere between threats and necessary dispensing of actual physical force—all he had to do was move the appropriate human chess pieces around until he was at the threshold of proclaiming checkmate. What little time he had spent in this land of plenty, he understood one basic factor that motivated these barbarians. From the lowest slug of a petty criminal all the way to the privileged elite, they all bowed before two gods.

Money and power.

Which equaled freedom, which translated into absolute power in their primitive minds. As they would say the more, the merrier.

It was a definite plus in his own power column, concerning his endgame to be exact, that the men he dealt with and controlled would never bite the hand that fed them, as long as that hand kept their bellies full and their numbered overseas accounts bulging. It also aided his cause to see their beds were warmed on certain nights by imported Asian beauties to keep carnal desires sated, while the agenda rolled ahead, smoothly and on target. With their needs met, he knew there was little room for whining, doubt, whatever negative energy might dump a wrench into the cogs of the coming juggernaut. Of course, the trump card, if all else failed, was a subtle reminder, now and again, of certain evidence he was armed with, involving everything from those ladies of questionable morals to high treason. Blackmail was always fair game, the last resort to keep the sun shining on his dreams.

But there was trouble and it was something he needed to address before it all unraveled and three years of laying the groundwork blew up in his face. The current problems in question might be many states away, but the backlash could well find him and his barbarian counterparts unless he started plugging up the holes before the whole dam cracked apart. Personal safety in a world of sabotage and subterfuge was always about as guaranteed, he thought, as the professed love of one of his call girls. Yes, he might be parked on a dark, empty prairie, somewhere between Tulsa and Oklahoma City, but he could sense some unknown danger headed his way.

Well, the right dose of paranoia could find him still breathing beyond any figurative or actual grenades lobbed his way.

He heard the man pulling up in his Land Rover, door

slamming, gruff voice barking out the indignation a moment later. "Hey, what the hell! Easy on the sheep-skin, Kim. The gun stays...why, you little..."

Chongjin smiled. The man was all bent out of shape as he was patted down for hidden minimikes, tape recorders and relieved of his holstered side arm. The American was threatening to kick ass all the way back to the thirty-eighth parallel, and so on.

Strange, he thought, how they still believed they could hold on to even a vestige of respect and dignity when they had sold out their own in the worst of trea-sonous acts.

The colonel checked his Rolex—the man late again for their third meeting in as many months. He ran his hands down the length of his cashmere coat. He smiled, enjoying both the feel of the fine Tibetan wool and the operative's foul mood and empty threats. He reached up and snapped on the low-wattage bulb. He wanted to view the face of his pawn—or potential nemesis, de-pending on the future— while reading the eyes for any hidden meaning behind the words. Likewise he was braced for some arrogant tirade, ready to verbally shoot down the man before he fired off a barrage of needless questions, designed simply to assuage his own guilt, lay his own worries to rest.

No time for small talk.

The side door was opened by one of his soldiers, the man from the Defense Intelligence Agency bounding his considerable bulk inside, plopping down in the seat directly opposite Chongjin. He scowled around the in-terior, as if he couldn't believe a foreigner was allowed the one simple perk of decent transportation by his own people. The van itself was customized, in fact, built by the DIA man's black-ops comrades on the sly. It was armor plated, meant to double as a rolling command center, complete with fax and computer modem, radio console with secured lines and police scanner, the whole superspy works hidden in the side paneling. With valid Oklahoma plates, all the necessary paperwork stashed in the glove box, even a lengthy background check by some suspicious redneck out there in the boondocks with gun and badge would find the vehicle traced back to a legitimate car dealership in Tulsa.

Perks.

When the door slid shut, the DIA man growled, "First, I don't like being ordered to clean up other people's messes, especially not after I warn the other guy about such a particular mess happening. And the next time one of your boys gives me a frisking like I'm some rat bastard flunkie, he'll be getting his next sushi fix through an IV. We clear?"

"Yes. We understand each other."

"I hope to hell so."

Even as his senses were pummeled by the winds of whiskey, Chongjin kept the smile in place, studied the DIA man he knew as Adam Turner. For some unclear, even borderline absurd reason the man insisted on dressing up as one of their cowboys of Western lore. From black Stetson, sheepskin coat, cowboy boots, down to the holster on his hip now empty of his pistol, he was something of a caricature of what he really was, which was a superoperative with access to all manner of classified intelligence and top-level clearance. Hardly the spit-and-polished picture of the many blacksuited covert operatives who were part of their organization. He was also a traitor to his own country. But the man seemed determined to play out the role of some rugged gunslinger, as if he wished his life were simply shrouded in myth and eccentricity. This was, indeed, Chongjin thought, a strange land, full of paradox and contradiction, an obscure subculture that mingled fact with fantasy, desire with reality. Like Turner, they were restless, never satisfied, always wishing to be something other than what they were, or to have more money and material things than they were already blessed with.

"Understand, my nerves aren't in the best of shape, Colonel."

"Yes. I can plainly smell that the pressure is getting to you."

The wide jaw clenched, the man grabbing the cowboy hat off his head, running an agitated hand through silver hair. "Is that supposed to be funny, Colonel?"

"I can assure you, nothing is amusing at the present."

"To understate the whole situation. Damn straight."

"Shall we get down to business? You know already I require a report from you on the progress I expected regarding the potential crisis."

"I guess you're talking about your sudden decision to use my man for something we didn't agree on in the beginning?"

Chongjin almost lost the smile, his patience thinning. "I don't like word games. You know what it is I want to hear. Let me explain this very simply. Your man is my man."

"Whom I brought out of a closet, one that is rattling full of his skeletons, and who has fulfilled already the one obligation he signed on for."

"Yes. And he did a superb job, if I understand correctly from our phone conversation, which my own people confirmed."

"Checking now to verify my sit-reps? Where's all the trust between us gone, Colonel? What happened to your 'we are the world' mantra?"

Chongjin ignored the barb. "Am I mistaken now or does he want an additional fee for his new services?"

"It's not the money, but depending on how the situation develops..."

Chongjin held up a hand. "Please. The detail about additional payment can be worked out. I assure him, through you, as I have assured you before. When we leave this country, all of you will have enough money to live out your lives in a style befitting royalty, better even than your Hollywood movie stars Americans seem so enthralled with. In a country, I might add, of your choosing. With new identities."

"As I was saying, it's not necessarily the money."

"What, then? Out with it."

"Part of the problem is, since it looks like a kidnapping, the FBI has already been called in."

"The way it was designed to appear."

"Not this soon. The risk factor, in other words, seems to be taking quantum leaps by the hour, Colonel. For one thing, your people, and my—our—man left behind the missile genius's little darling. In the interests of time, they bailed before they could find her."

Chongjin kept smiling, noted the scowl on Turner's face. His expression, he sensed, was both mystifying and infuriating to the American. "I see no problem in that regard. So she talks to the FBI. There will be no ransom demand. Their FBI will sit around, staring at a phone that will never ring. And since the human cargo, as we and our organization outlined, will be delivered here by truck in no more than twenty-four hours, it would appear that all systems are go."

"Not so fast. My—our—man hasn't exactly endeared himself to certain folks in the intelligence community. If they think he's loose on American soil, he might find himself getting bagged before he nails down the big scores you ordered. Songbird. Witness Protection Program. Fingers aimed our way."

"So, you have told me all of this before. Refresh my memory. You have called this wonder assassin what?"

"The Reaper."

"Yes. As in the Grim Reaper." Chongjin felt his smile widen. Perhaps his first assessment of Turner wasn't entirely accurate. Propaganda and myth didn't contain themselves within the boundaries of any one country, restrict the lies and half truths of bravado to any single culture. Like America, his own country reveled in shrouding itself in myth, even spun out bald-faced lies, glorifying men of rank and power when and where it suited those in charge of the masses. That was particularly true, he thought, of the present leader, an obese drunkard and lecher who required a steady diet of Viagra just to feed the myth of his so-called sexual prowess. In Chongjin's personal but silent estimation, Kim Jong Il was far from anything glorious or even worthy of the first scintilla of respect. Sad but true, even his country, he had admit to himself, had serious problems, due in large part to who held the reins of power at the very top.

The current son and the deceased father had both

made the masses believe they were gods to be revered. The starving peasants in the desolate countryside actually believing stories of how they had come down from the heavens on chariots of fire to rule and to lead the Korean people to glory and greatness. It was a known fact that the peasants believed Kim Il and now Kim Jong were actually responsible for the sun rising and setting. He often wondered about the sanity of his own countrymen, swallowing such childish nonsense. It was also aimed at brainwashing those who were too miserable and wretched to know, or to want any better. In time, he would change all of that. In time, he planned to drink a bottle of Kim Jong's imported cognac, over his dead body.

For a brief moment, aware of how highly regarded this Reaper had come to him, he tried to conjure up an image of this superassassin he had never seen. He pictured some gaunt, steely-eyed killer who probably, in all reality, had shot more unarmed or unsuspecting men in the back than anything else. The fabled Grim Reaper, that skeletal figure cloaked in black, but wielding a pistol instead of a scythe, coming in the dead of night to take lives at the appointed hour.

Chongjin dropped the smile. "Kindly and with brevity explain what you think the problem is."

"Okay, you want succinct. One of your recruits out of Baghdad went crazy this morning, slaughtered fifty-something New Yorkers on a subway train, including cops, before he blew himself up for the glory of Allah. That kind of body count tends to draw attention. Not to mention cops get kind of pissed off when other cops get killed. They get this vendetta thing in their heads."

"I ordered the removal of his next of kin, which was successful."

"And you informed me a while ago you already ordered your own people to hand any remaining cleanup over to *our* man. Meaning you've still got a full cell of Iraqis, probably already have word the Iraqi and family were waxed, and now have a full head of steam. Wondering who they can trust. Wondering if they just shouldn't go ahead and act out their wildest jihad fantasies. Let me further spell out the problem. One of your recruits bulls ahead of the program meant to secure our own bailing out as a ruse, or a trump card to hold back a potential armada of F-15s, stealths, whatever. Maybe, as we speak, not only the New York cell, but the other two cells, are locked and loaded, ready to hit the streets and take out as many infidels as they can. All this, worst case, well before I've secured our ride out of the country. Problem two. Our man is now putting himself on the front line to clean up the garbage before it gets any messier."

"So, he is already in New York?"

"Yes, Colonel, he's there. He has the scent and he's moving in, as we speak, to start the bloodbath. Another item—he's not going in solo. Meaning he's brought his own handpicked crew. What I'm saying, Colonel, New York is set to go hot. War."

"I'm still not seeing the problem."

"Goddamit. Reaper's face has been around the block. He's a freelancer, bouncing around from every alphabet-soup agency from here to Tombouctou. I'm talking wet work that would make anything you could produce in your neck of the woods—"

"Enough. You are concerned this Reaper or one of his operatives will be picked up by the FBI."

"And he knows about our organization, through both of our cutouts, since some of the recruitment came from my end. The man's not stupid. He wants to know who's buttering his bread and why. I believe he knows at least some of the score, since he's already versed in some of the finer points of the drill."

"Meaning he knows more than he should."

"Meaning he has his own ways of accessing information. Not even I have a full scorecard of who's on the team or who has said what exactly to who. Or maybe he and a few other guys are running around now, thinking they, too, could be expendables like the Iraqis they're marched in to eliminate. No payday for them? Well, maybe they have something on disk, copies of what they think they know about our own gig stashed all over God only knows where."

"Is he or any of his operatives aware of our immediate end game in this country?"

"Not that I'm aware of. The bottom line here, Colonel, is I've marched in my loose cannons to knock your loose cannons from Baghdad off the deck."

Chongjin kept his anger in check at the American's impertinence. "I understand the predicament. It was an unfortunate miscalculation on my part, regarding the depth of rage and hatred of my chosen cannon fodder. I didn't anticipate one of them becoming so impatient."

"You agree we could have a serious situation ready to blow up all to hell in our faces?"

"I'm telling you to stick to the original plan. No war was ever won, Mr. Turner, by not overcoming some adversity. Crisis breeds character, if a man has any character to begin with."

"Speaking of adversity, there's something else we need to discuss. Such as getting coordinated on the final leg of the logistics."

"Twenty-four hours, the major flies. It is very simple."

"Whoa..."

"Make it happen. I won't tolerate excuses or failure."

"So, when it hits the fan, you think we all just go skipping off into the sunset, no chance of a Sidewinder or Sparrow or even a Tomahawk come streaking up our collective ass. You know something else, I don't like being kept in the dark like this at the eleventh hour. Like I said, I don't even know the faces of all the players on the team."

"You will know them when the time comes."

"Yeah? How?"

Chongjin let the smile come back. "They will be the ones who are not shooting at you."

"Colonel, do you hear me laughing?"

Chongjin kept the smile. "Do your job. That's what you're paid for."

"You know, I almost bailed, skipped out on this madness."

"Really? You must reconsider your moments of sobriety. When you begin thinking too much, I suggest another shot of whiskey."

"Ha-ha. Too late for all of that, Colonel. I'm smart enough, or too scared of dying, I'm not sure which. I took your money. You have the pictures. I'm in to the finish line, for better or worse."

"I have more than a few dirty pictures of you in various unsavory scenarios. When you drink yourself to stupidity and carelessness, then fornicate, you should be careful how much classified information you are willing to divulge to a mere whore. Whores are likewise notorious thieves."

"I'll keep that in mind, Colonel, the next time you send Jun or Su Kim or whatever her name is to ply me with drinks."

Chongjin could feel his face flush with anger. "When this is finished and we are on our way with the other human cargo, you will have all the whores and whiskey you desire." He watched the American for any sudden moves as he slowly slipped a hand into his coat, withdrew a fat white envelope and dumped it in the man's lap. "There. That should put some steel into your backbone." Chongjin saw something dangerous flicker in the American's eyes as he hefted the envelope, tucked it away inside his coat. "You're welcome."

"You know, because of the coming program's finale, we're both aware I know a couple of the men in the so-called council. Contact with them has been unavoidable. I'm telling you they're fanatics, Colonel, bad if not worse than your Iraqi recruits. They're in this for more than just money or a good time or securing some tropical paradise where they can live out their golden years, scratching their bikini briefs."

"I am aware of the motivations of the men in the Phoenix Council. Their goals coincide with my own. If, however, in the future they begin to conflict..." He paused. "Again. Do your job. You'll have the necessary assistance inside the compound."

"The way you say that, I hear a threat between the lines."

"I don't threaten. I deliver. I produce results. I will contact you at some point within the next twelve hours. I'll want another situation report. My people and members of the council will soon be gathering at this cowboy farm—"

"Ranch house," Turner interrupted.

"Whatever. I, for one, am tired of living in cheap motels."

"That's your choice, considering all the cash you've thrown around."

"That money does not necessarily come from me."

"You're telling me the Iraqi leader has financed this operation from his pilfered oil billions."

"I'm telling you as much as you need to know. I'm telling you to make happen what you have been paid an outrageous sum for."

"Oh, I'll make it happen. Just ask yourself what if a squad of American fighter jets wants to blow us out of the sky?"

"Mr. Turner, this operation has not been put together, at considerable expense and risk to my own life, for me to come to your country and commit suicide." Chongjin's face turned to stone. He looked away, finished with this American who came to him practically bursting apart with doubt and anxiety. He didn't know it yet, of course, but Chongjin had no intention of keeping his promise of delivering a paradise of whores, booze and cash to this man. He looked forward to killing this American himself.

"That will be all for now. My men will see to it your

gun and your flask are returned to you on the way out."
He could feel that look again, boring into him through
the shaft of light. He pinned Turner with a cold measuring gaze of his own, then the American was up and
opening the door.

It was good to be alone at last, the colonel thought,
free from the face of weakness, the stink of whiskey and
fear. He needed time to think, puzzle through the logistics, work it out in his mind before he addressed the
council and the soldiers who would perform the real
dirty work.

There was much to do in the coming hours before he
initiated the first act of the plan. If every man who was
bought and paid for did his job, they would all succeed.
If someone squawked, bailed, ran to the military authorities in some weak attempt to save himself...

To fail was unthinkable. If he failed at this late stage,
it would simply mean he would die in this land of barbarians. That abhorrent notion alone, he hoped, should
be enough to see him pull off the first of many grim
chores to come.

The endgame was only just beginning.

THE FBI CREDENTIALS were every bit as phony as the
good senator's public charade. "Special Agent" Armand
Geller knew so much about the boy wonder's double
life, this ballyhooed Democrat's poster phenom as the
Mr. Family Man-Captain America of the new century,
it was all he could to keep from puking.

The man's life was a whopping fat sham. Welcome,
he thought, to politics.

Well, the scam was gaining momentum on two

fronts, both crucibles heating up, in fact, for the men who doled out the lion's share of campaign contributions to the fine senator from Oklahoma. And the coming scorching heat the men of the Phoenix Council were about to unleash was why he had come to the man's gilded cowboy palace on the prairie.

After having zapped the entire security system, he was now sitting in the senator's study, marveling at the wonders of inheritance. From his seated post in the leather-bound swivel chair behind a teakwood desk the size of most offices, he took in the sprawling opulence, all of it handed down to the only son, courtesy of the old man, who had been the last of the cattle barons out there. Some hefty petro bucks had likewise assisted nicely in paving the boy wonder's golden road, Old Man Winston having finagled his way into the state's oil boom when the good times were rolling. Before the last gusher had sputtered out, the Sterling fortune was reckoned in the neighborhood of ten billion and change, climbing every day, of course, on interest alone.

That was then.

When the old man kicked off from liver failure, notorious for his love of Jack Daniel's, their fortune could have fed Somalia and Ethiopia combined for a decade to come. The main vacuum for the bucks was the kid, who, incredible as it sounded, had squandered vast sums on bad investments and a closet playboy Shambala until he was down to a paltry twelve million. Then there was the first marriage, shot to hell, because the only son couldn't keep his pants zipped up. Then the always helpful and concerned tribe of lawyers marched in, making sure the fair offended damsel was generously mollified, lest she go public with a scandal. Then there was a private Lear, a Rolls-Royce, his own political meteor ride to the top, which required more siphoning of dough....

And the good folks of Oklahoma seemed to have forgiven him every bit of his foolishness and indulgence, chalking it up to "boys will be boys." Not only that, the Democrats were parading him around now to be their man of the hour for the next presidential election.

Only in America.

The kid still had plenty of toys left, and Geller felt a tad of envy flaming up as he scanned the room. Video games were spread around the massive study. Pool table in the adjoining game room, indoor pool, hot tub. And then there were the trophies—stuffed elk, black bear, musk ox, bighorn, all bagged, of course, by Pops Sterling.

Geller swiveled around, grinning up at the regal figure looming on the wall. The oil painting, he guessed, was fifteen by six, if it was an inch. Old Winston Sterling, looking majestic in a surly sort of way, long black frock coat, frilly cowboy shirt, with an old Springfield rifle clutched at port arms in big, raw-boned hands. The picture of rugged individualism, Mr. Wild West himself.

He heard the senator scuffling beyond double doors. Geller had already found the stainless-steel .45-caliber Colt in Sterling's top drawer. It made him wonder just how nervous Darren Sterling had become, or if the piece was being reserved, a .45-caliber round his last meal if all his present woes came crawling like vipers out of the hole to bite him on the ass.

He was leaning back, chucking the cannon up and down a few times, when he called out, "In here, Senator."

Geller was smiling, eyeing the pistol when he felt the man moving in, his wife calling out from somewhere, wondering what was going on. He heard him inform her he had been expecting a late-night guest, the silky voice smoothing it over, kindly asking her to return to bed.

The doors were closing, the lawmaker demanding, "Who—? How did you...?"

He went silent, noting a stranger was in possession of his gun, a man in black sitting in his chair, half-smiling but solemn, looking as if he was the harbinger of bad news and very bad news.

Which, Geller knew, was to a large extent true.

Geller looked up, measuring the man. The robe was bulging some in the midriff, indicating the senator liked his calories as much as he did his Korean prostitutes. Sterling, he noted, was doing some sizing up of his own, and plainly nervous about the view. Understandable, since Geller knew the senator was looking at quite the contrast. Where Sterling was soft, with a mane of white hair neatly coiffed from hundred-dollar styling jobs, Geller was a lean, mean SOB. He saw the senator balking at the sight of a skeletal face that looked carved by an ax, military-issue buzz cut, a high forehead that was mottled with purple splotches from some adversary's near miss with flying lead. Where Geller knew he was a killer, a warrior, the senator was little more than a walking pile of bullshit he'd just as soon step around.

But duty called, and the council had appointed the man to tighten the noose, iron out a few matters that needed to be brought to the senator's attention.

The guy was checking the alarm box on the wall, when Geller called out, "You're going to need another system."

"What did you do to it?"

Geller produced a small black box from inside his leather jacket. He smiled at the instrument, about the size of a cell phone. "Amazing what some of those guys at NSA can do."

"Is that what you are? An intelligence operative from the National Security Agency?"

"This thing emits a laser beam," Geller said, "a transference of heat, invisible to the naked eye. You don't want to get in front of this thing when it's turned on, I understand. Heat something like two thousand degrees Fahrenheit, light a guy up like a Roman candle, or so they say. Right before I called and woke you and the little lady up—extend my apologies to her, will you—to let you know we needed to chat, all I had to do was aim it at your surveillance camera out front, and the heat actually ripples through the whole system. Probably melted the guts of your whole main box to jelly. Oh, and you're also going to need a new pane of glass on the door leading out to the gazebo."

"What the—? My wife thought there was an intruder on the grounds. How am I going to explain any of this?"

Geller shrugged. "Just do what you do best, Senator. Lie."

The politician was stepping toward his desk, flacid features hardening best they could. "If you're here to try to intimidate me—"

Geller stopped the guy in midstride when he slowly trained the muzzle crotchward. "That's exactly what

I'm here to do." Geller took the sheaf of papers from another pocket, flung them on the desk. When the senator grabbed them, and before he could start squawking, Geller went on, "You can keep those. I helped myself to your laser printer on the way in. Amazing. You went from riches to rags, and now you're back to riches again. Look at those whopping offshore account numbers. Dummy companies, assumed identities." He whistled, the chuckle all rolling bass. "Made in the shade, son. Does the little missus know how much cash you have lying around?"

"What is it you want?"

"I also have some rather interesting pictures of you and a lady friend—I believe her name is Su Lin?" He saw the flash of anger wrestling against the shame in his eyes.

The guy was shaking now, but seemed unable to move, take his eyes off the gun aimed at his family jewels. "Do you mind? You're making me..."

"Nervous? Sorry. That is kind of rude of me." He chuckled, smiled, lost the look and put an edge to his voice as he set the pistol in front of him. "Here's the short and the bitter. I was sent here by some very powerful men to remind you that your soul has already been bought and paid for. You are going to return to the Hill. There is a certain bill your colleagues have been trying to grease up and slide through."

"Concerning normalizing relations with North Korea? The exchange program of technology if the North Koreans agree to go less militant?"

"You are going to fight it, make the stand, charm the pants off them, whatever you have to do or say to make folks think you've lost your marbles."

The lawmaker was a scripted act, Geller comparing him to a used-car salesman, always on the con, looking to schmooze it out until he had the upper hand. Sterling fell into the contrived role he was famous for in front of the cameras or the Sunday-morning talking-head shows. "Let me speak quite frankly here. There are a few points on that matter that never fit, which I strongly urge you to reconsider. I suggest we take a look at the whole picture first before I attempt to sell..."

"I understand your dilemma."

"How can I be expected to take some hawkish stand that's completely out of character with my party's position on North Korea?"

"Senator," Geller said, rising and sidling a few feet to the side. "You are on our need-to-know leash. Period. The beauty of it is that in a matter of days, perhaps even less, your contradictory position is going to make you a hero. You are going to be leading the pack, a genius, no less, who gets to shout out loud, 'I told you so.'"

"It still doesn't make sense."

"Where you're concerned, it doesn't need to. The Senate is split nearly in half on this package. You are part of the Committee on Foreign Intelligence, head of a subcommittee that deals with relations between the U.S. and both Koreas. This much I will tell you. Several of your esteemed colleagues have become fallen angels like yourself, their own wings so badly soiled, a few are worse off than what we have on you, if you can believe such a thing. They are playing ball with the people I represent or else certain embarrassing matters go before the public forum. No names at this time, but let's just say the real power I represent has proof of various improprieties involving interns, page boys, like that. We even have the dirt on one of your colleagues who enjoys huffing up a little cocaine now and then."

"Preposterous!"

"It's fact. By the way, I suggest you pack up, Darren. You're going to want to be out of this neighborhood anyway. Send the little lady on a long trip while you're at it."

"What does that mean?"

"Once you're back in Washington, you will be contacted with further instructions." Geller walked out from behind the desk, the lawmaker glancing from the gun to his course. He almost hoped the guy went for it, give him an excuse to put his Glock .45ACP to work. "Oh, and Su Lin? She'll be at the Ramada at Tysons, just in case you get the itch. Under the name Jane Fonda." Sterling didn't get the humor, the guy all but locked up in the misery of his own creation. "I'll show myself out."

"And that's it?"

"For now."

4

The third sighting of the black van kicked the Executioner into high alert. It was lights-out this time around, as the vehicle swung off Atlantic Avenue and eased into an alley between the Lebanese taverna on the FBI's hot list and a chain of apartment buildings gone to seed.

"No drive-by this time. And that's not one of ours. What do you think?"

"Not sure," Bolan said.

"Third time's the charm? Those windows, by the way, are illegally tinted. The more I watch this place, the bigger knot I get in my gut. Guys coming and going. Same guys, like they're out for a stroll, wanting to check the sights, see who's watching the store. Stroll back in, report to the boss."

Bolan had plenty of thoughts on the subject, but kept quiet in the shotgun seat of the Crown Victoria. A heightened sense of combat readiness always put the soldier in a mode to let actions do the talking for him. On the other hand, Special Agent Marcus Broadwater seemed to feel the need to hear his own voice, whether from bottled adrenaline, too much coffee or muscles stiff from hours of being cramped behind the wheel on both roving and sitting surveillance, Bolan couldn't say. He went on to inform Bolan a number of items the soldier already knew. Such as the late hour, a full house of Arabs still inside the restaurant. Such as the day's rousting of the occupants inside, meant to sweat any guilty ones into showing a dirty hand or head for the nearest subway for slaughter act two.

So far no takers for an absolute revelation that there was a terrorist congregation holed up in the block's favorite Mideast eatery.

Up to that point too many hours had hung floating in limbo, but the soldier had a gut churning over with a familiar grim anticipation it was about to hit the fan. Without fail, waiting was always something of a grueling test before the action kicked in to separate the givers from the takers in the ultimate of exams. He was armed with his trusty Beretta 93-R in shoulder rigging for starters, if and when the terror dragons starting breathing fire his way. The .44 Magnum Desert Eagle, tied down on his hip, was visible enough beneath the tail of his loose-fitting windbreaker to have drawn more than a passing curious eye from Broadwater. And what was stashed away in the nylon war bag in the Crown Vic's trunk definitely bucked the standards for field hardware outlined in the Justice manual. Uzi submachine gun, enough extra clips to field a full squad of commandos charging an enemy's door, and that was just for warm-ups. Throw in a pouch stuffed with an assortment of frag, flash-stun and incendiary grenades, a SPAS-12 autoshotgun to boot, twenty pounds of C-4 just in case. Any reasonable homegrown G-man would wonder if

Special Agent Belasko hadn't come to New York to start full-scale urban war.

Then there was a combat harness and blacksuit, the Marine Ka-bar knife in a sheath around his lower leg, if he needed a silent, up-close takedown or two on the way in to the real room-clearing butcher's work. Aside from the killing goodies, Brognola had handed Bolan the keys to his own safehouse, a brownstone in trendy Brooklyn Heights. There, the soldier had access to spare weapons, a sat-link with fax modem, all the high-tech toys to keep him tied to the big Fed and Stony Man Farm.

Many hours ago all the details were ironed out to get the soldier there, ready and waiting as dawn crept around the corner. After a military shuttle to JFK, the soldier had been whisked by a Justice courier to a joint special task force in a Brooklyn office. No one on the home team had much to go on. Standard briefings had earlier struck Bolan as next to window dressing over the real problem, as far as any decent leads that would land them on the doorstep of whatever terrorists in hiding remained in the cell. If there was a cell.

Call it bureaucratic wrangling. Tag it as the wheels of promotion turning faster than a lower-ranking agent's pay raise, or simply folks at the top of the hierarchy a little gun-shy as they had hot flashes of careers getting flushed down the old toilet if they bulled ahead and made the tough call, afraid of stepping on toes connected to ass they might have kiss the next day. Whatever, some doubt, incredible as it sounded, echoed down the rank and file about the existence of a terror machine getting itself gassed up to go on high-octane hate.

Bolan decided to stick with the grunts, the kind of men who usually had their noses chasing the scent on the street, running on a hunch provided him by a few special agents he handpicked to assist him in combing the perimeters of any hives swarming with possible lunatics poised to burn down half of New York. The gist of it from his chosen foot soldiers, he recalled, was that the Lebanese taverna was where one of the day's two mystery Arab casualties had worked as a waiter. The FBI had marched in the local health inspectors, the INS going to bat next, all of it designed to rattle cages or get the fishing expedition started with a few choice pieces of chum tossed into a suspected pool of human sharks. Then, while the nerves were still jangling from top to bottom, the Feds weighed in behind the whole mass of officialdom to grill and drill the owner and various and sundry employees and their families. It was borderline unconstitutional, letting the insinuations the Arab-Americans knew more than they were telling hang like a radioactive cloud. But given the day's horrific slaughter on a commuter train, with NYPD blue howling for justified vengeance and the families of the victims demanding answers, the FBI had taken off the gloves. According to his ride, every single Arab male they questioned at the Lebanese taverna was nervous, evasive as hell on many of the finer points during Q and A. That alone didn't mean much, but then every single passport checked them out as either Jordanian or Lebanese nationals. And in Bolan's hard experience, if there was nothing to hide, why all the irradiated nerves and talking out of both sides of the mouth? He hadn't been on hand for the FBI's session on attitude readjustment, but Broadwater's synopsis and personal gut feeling led him to strongly suspect they were right now where the action was.

Or about to go down.

The husky black agent kept his sights trained on the darkened restaurant facade. "Notice you don't say much. Can't be the company you keep, since you asked for me yourself."

Bolan said nothing.

"I get the impression, Special Agent Belasko," he said, using Bolan's alias, "you're not real big on this partner thing. Something telling me we're not destined to be a Glover and Gibson act."

"Nothing personal."

Broadwater sounded off a grunt that could have meant anything or nothing. Whatever the man's sentiment, Bolan had nothing but the highest regard for any law-enforcement official, federal or otherwise. Unless he missed his guess, an elimination game was on the table. The stakes were about to go off the chart, with unknown killers moving in to storm the taverna. He could be sure Broadwater, the FBI and Justice agents on stakeout detail had wives and families to think about beyond the job. Risk, of course, and the possibility of the ultimate sacrifice were always inherent when it came down to lawmen performing their duty, tracking and corraling the bad guys, even in the line of fire. Bolan wasn't looking to cowboy the play. But he didn't intend to see any personal assistance provided him by the FBI and Justice, courtesy of Brognola's standing order, thrown into a firefight that would see them leaving behind grieving widows and fatherless children. Plain and sim-

ple, Bolan wanted his team there for field intelligence
and support. The Executioner knew he was the one best
suited to do any shooting, if a gunfight erupted. He figured Broadwater wouldn't especially cater to what he
might see as a patronizing or arrogant point of view, so
Bolan kept the line of thought to himself.

The soldier began thinking he might have to crash
through the front door, bulldoze in to take care of business the old-fashioned way. "When you were there earlier, what was the layout?"

Broadwater's brow creased, hinting at a frown, the
man obviously not caring to be the one doing all the giving. "Dining room, wall-to-wall bar on the west side.
Posh and spacious spread all around. No expert, but I
caught a view of some of the Mideast trimmings, down
to a hanging scimitar, some kind of golden bull smack
in the middle of main dining, like something maybe the
ancient Babylonians would pray to. Ambiance, who
knows. Kitchen was your standard stainless steel, walk-
ins, freezer, like that. Back room, though, made me
think we had something a little more than your usual
mom-and-pop dining establishment feeding the regular
Arab American clientele."

"How so?"

"They had the backgammon boards out in plain sight,
but they have a long table in there, couple dozen chairs
scattered around, everything looking too neat and clean
for appearance's sake. I'm thinking the back room is for
war council."

Likewise that was Bolan's take. "You said there were
families upstairs?"

"Right."

"How many women and children?"

"Didn't take a head count, but it looked like they could have packed half of Beirut upstairs just over the dining room. Place was renovated about two years ago. I found out Lebanese contractors did all the additions. From the outside itself, it looks like half an apartment complex fanning out from the restaurant. Inside...who knows? The way it feels to me, I'm thinking maybe somebody had in mind all along to bring over half their country."

"What else?"

"Like what?"

"Did you go upstairs? Go inside any storerooms? Maybe a room that didn't look like it quite belonged there in what you called a war council?"

Bolan was thinking weapons cache, some hidden chamber that housed a communications layout.

"We weren't exactly armed with a search warrant."

"Gotcha."

"The judge did sign off for a phone tap."

"That call to Chicago, you mentioned."

"Right. Traced it to a pay phone on Fifty-ninth near Midway Airport. Another call, two hours ago from here. Again a pay phone, this one on the other side of town near the University of Chicago. You know this already. Mind me asking what you're thinking?"

"I'm thinking somebody needs to alert the Chicago field office. I'm thinking problems."

"This whole town's already under the military equivalent of ThreatCon Delta. Silent alarm, that is, security beefed up from the Statue of Liberty, clear out to Plum Island Animal Disease Center, I'm told. Chicago's already gotten the bad vibes we're feeling about those two calls. Right now I'm more worried about my hometown. If this thing is about some terrorist cells reaching from here to Chicago...that is what you're implying?"

"Something tells me we're about to find out, Agent Broadwater. Pop the trunk for me, will you?"

"Where you off to?"

"Taking a walk."

"By yourself?"

"Right."

"And leave me to keep the meter running?"

"I'll stay in touch."

"What the hell am I, Belasko, just overpaid taxi service?"

Bolan kept his look neutral. "Stay put unless you hear otherwise. Have the other units fan out, make it about two blocks apart, and sit tight. All units on Tac One. You and me on Tac Two."

Broadwater muttered something to himself, but knew better than to push it, since the field director had handed down orders that came straight from the Justice Department.

Bolan was out the door, the trunk popping up. He decided to skip the harness, but made himself ready to go full tactical just the same. The Uzi came out of the war bag first, a small nylon pouch up and slung next over the soldier's shoulder, stuffed with spare 40-round clips in 9 mm Parabellum. One frag, one flash-stun grenade dumped into the pocket of his windbreaker. He checked the narrow maw of an alley that would allow him to approach the taverna from the east side at the back. The Executioner chambered the first round in the Uzi, ignored Broadwater's scowl and headed across the street. It was little more than the usual gut feeling, but it was a rare solar eclipse when combat instinct let Bolan down.

Stoked for this slice of predawn Brooklyn to blow into a noisy crucible of hell on earth, the Executioner gathered momentum and melted into the momentarily friendly cloak of the deep shadows.

HUSAT AL-MAHLID HEARD the voice of the North Korean colonel invading his own angry thoughts as he listened to the squawking around him.

"I thought they were supposed to protect us! Not slaughter our friends and their families if they believed they would be exposed to American authorities!"

And the voice floated in, taking him back in time.

"Take heed. The waiting for word from my end may fray your nerves, perhaps turn some of you against the others. One of you may even decide his life and the lives of his very family are more important than the mission...."

His memories was interrupted by his colleagues.

"I agree with Mushadah. Our alleged benefactors have become more of a threat to our lives than those FBI crows who descended on us today."

"And what is to become of all of us now that the North Koreans see us as liabilities? Will they march in their ninja assassins in the middle of the night to execute us in turn?"

"Many of us have families. I, for one, do not care if I martyr myself, but if I wanted to see my family butchered, I could have remained in Iraq, wandering about, risking a laser-guided bomb from the American buzzards!"

Dangerous talk. Even though they squabbled among themselves in Arabic, Mahlid was aware the FBI jackals were clever enough to have wired the room when they had strolled around earlier, wearing their collective mask of indifference, grunting out some cool appraisal of the area, but he knew better. They couldn't hide their suspicion. It rang through, the clang of a death knell, in every question they had put to them.

"That Hasab did what he did is no fault of his own."

"He was tired of waiting. Wondering. Worrying."

"Each of us is committed to jihad, but I won't sit still while the Koreans who have proclaimed allegiance to our own cause circle in like buzzards for the feast."

"Then what are we to do?"

"We take up arms and march out into the streets."

"I agree. But what if, like Hasab, we are martyred before our time in the eyes of the Koreans! These dogs have proved treacherous. Our families shouldn't be marked for execution, murdered in a foreign land like Saddam's family."

"It is a blasphemous thing indeed for these foreigners to slay our families."

"Allah will not forgive us if we allow our families to be killed by vipers who view us as nothing but an albatross to their plans."

"And what, may I ask, is this great plan of theirs?"

Mahlid closed his eyes, drawing on his cigarette. As was his right and duty, he claimed the seat at the head of the table. This was a war council, a gathering of holy warriors, all of them sworn to a sacred duty, prepared long ago to sacrifice their own lives, committed solely to taking fifty or more infidel eyes for every eye plucked by American vultures during the Gulf War. Only now it was all beginning to sound more to him like one of those wretched American talk shows where infidel families screeched and cursed each other over sins of the flesh. Perhaps, he thought, America had contaminated their souls, the tough hide of the warriors he once knew sloughed off like so much shedding of a snake, baring now some underlying weakness due to exposure of this land's many cursed temptations and contradictions.

As their chosen leader, he could indulge the squawking up to a point. At the moment he viewed himself much like a father would quietly referee bickering between sons, hoping they could resolve their differences or put aside their fear and anger on their own before he stepped up and started the serious backhanding. For one, he knew far more details on the mission than the others, but he had been warned to keep many secrets to himself. Loose talk and backbiting would serve no purpose now but to guarantee some reckless course of action.

He was one of the first to be funneled through Lebanon, a country, he knew, that had become a factory for phony passports, visas and the exporting of freedom fighters through certain prearranged filter channels designed by various intelligence agencies. Getting in wasn't the problem, nor was building the false fronts of lives as humble immigrants seeking only a slice of the pie that was the so-called American dream. When they arrived here, yes, their role was to play out the honest and diligent pursuit of a better way of life. It was all, of course, simply a ruse leading to judgment day. Had he known then what he knew now, though, he would have demanded up front from their sponsors a guaranteed concession that if one of their own did something to jeopardize the mission, they would handle it on their own.

Twenty-nine men, including himself, were Tikritis, hailing from Iraq's desert soil. He wondered what the great leader would think now if he could hear them clucking about like so many old hens. It was disgraceful. There was more blood on the hands of these men than perhaps the entire Republican Guard or the special-forces brigades had shed during the rape of Kuwait. He opened his eyes, peering into the hanging clouds of cigarette smoke, hoping his extended bout of silence would calm the anxious talk.

"We have been abandoned. Our enemies are now anyone who is outside this room."

So much for patience.

He knew them all by name, deed and prior life. Abdullah and Jabal were in the cleansing business after the war against the infidels, gassing countless sprawling Kurdish villages so thoroughly that it was believed every living thing, down to plant life, or a scorpion in its hole, had been wiped off the face of the desert. Muhmad and Mohammed were the personal executioners in the service. They shot generals dead in cabinet meetings, or pumped a wayward son-in-law full of bullets on the whim of their leader himself. So Mahlid understood, then, how execution could become the order of the day, when treachery and backstabbing walked the shadows, hand in hand. A part of him understood the thinking of the North Koreans, how certain messes, once made, could only be cleaned up with one degree of finality. Still, he wasn't about to sit by and watch the foreigners butcher his own people in this filthy land.

A moment of silence was on the verge of dropping over the room as Mahlid found several of the elders looking his way, as if noticing him for the first time, waiting now on words of wisdom. A few of the younger Tikritis babbled on, but their voices trailed off as heads swiveled about, nervous hands toyed with cigarettes, lifted coffee cups. Granted, he was feeling the heat of his own paranoia, having sounded the alarm himself, but keeping up appearances while so doing. In calm and orderly fashion, he removed every pistol, subgun or rocket launcher, every brick of plastic explosive from different hiding spots around the restaurant. Some had chosen to keep pistols and subguns within easy grasp on the table, as if fearing the vaunted FBI would come crashing through the door any moment, while the bulk of the mother lode was heaped at the base of the wall. The fact that the duffel bags that would carry the weapons and explosives through the city were now gathered in the room should have told them he had already made his decision. Perhaps they simply needed a reminder of who and what they were, reassurance beefing up faltering nerve from the voice of authority.

"I am disappointed in what I am hearing." He wandered a disapproving eye down the table as the younger ones fidgeted with cups and cigarettes, glancing about as if believing their self-appointed Mahdi must be referring to someone else. "We are of the Tikriti clan. It is believed we are related to the very blood of our great leader. We are men, we are warriors, not a bunch of old hags fretting about matters which cannot be changed. Not even Allah, it has been said, can change the past. Hasab did what he did, and he has gone already to his reward. Now..." He paused, the elder lion about to rise up among the pride, the passion for the hunt building a storm in his eyes. "It has always been my call to make and I have made the decision. Our actions will affect our families, but I pray and I believe in my heart Allah will protect and provide for them. What we are going to do will also see grave consequences for the other cells beyond this city. I can only pray for them, that they, too, see that we must not become puppets of fate dictated by the whims of the Koreans. No more. I believe the other cells will take initiative, knowing in their hearts that we didn't come to this country to die for whatever is the cause of the Koreans. We didn't come to this accursed land of jackals and vipers to see our jihad fail. The time has come. In a few short minutes we will leave here and go meet our holy destiny. You will be allowed to pray one last time. You won't be allowed to say goodbye to your families lest they wail and gnash their teeth and attempt to change your hearts."

He stabbed out the cigarette, his wide nostrils flaring, the great bull riled up. "We will leave here in twos and threes. We will look at the map of this city, and I will grant each of you a target of your choosing. Remember, after what Hasab did, the police will be out everywhere. They wear body armor. They may attempt to shoot you on sight, since this country seems to think," he said, and smiled, "all of us are crazed terrorists. I suggest," he said, recalling vaguely what the Korean colonel had told them, "when you see a policeman you shoot first. Shoot for the head. If that is unsuccessful, I don't believe their body armor covers the groin area or the legs. Let us rise, let us pray to Allah for success and for glory in his name. And then we will prepare to leave. Our war against the Great Satan has only just begun."

5

His real name was Robert Bowen, and normally he loved New York. It was a big, mean, dirty mother of a town.

New York had attitude.

In terms of sprawl, population density and the total sweet ambiance of rampant desperate criminal intent in all five boroughs, he had to rank it up there with, say, Mexico City, Calcutta, Bangkok. The nice thing about urban jungles, he knew, there was always work for the freelancing disposal artist with his degree of talent, not to mention plenty of places to hide the bodies. Another plus about concrete battlefields was general civilian apathy, that see-no-evil act after the violence and mayhem, so muddied or doctored up by conflicting eyewitness accounts that homicide detectives were usually left shaking their heads.

Despite the call now over the secured line, forced to soothe tweaked nerves at the worst possible time, he briefly hashed over the good old days, wishing to hell and back it could all be what it once was.

Clean and simple.

When the Five Families owned the town, lock, stock and barrel, he thought. When graft and corruption was the accepted routine from city hall down to a beat cop with alimony and six kids. Back then, when cash got tight, or the CIA brass was feeling its knees buckle before some Senate Committee on Intelligence and black ops went under a political microscope, he'd struck out on his own, used his considerable skills in the disposal business to help those New Yorkers who could help him.

Of course, that was the past. The present New York wasn't offering too many attractive propositions. He needed to get refocused, or his final view of the town would be from behind bars, if he even got that lucky. No amount of wistful yearning and recollection of past bloodshed, bodies dumped in the East River and numbered accounts swimming in six figures would steer them to the other side of the job ahead.

The voice on the cell phone was a reminder of where the line began to blur when it came down to national security, every shade in between black ops and standard military operations. Spookdom always wanted instant results, no delays, no excuses, especially when the heat was cranked up on their rear ends. A hit like this took time, planning and an exit strategy, none of which he had. It was straight bulldoze work, and he was thinking his original asking price of a cool million was next to minimum wage. Naturally he'd siphoned off the lion's share for this outing, handing a quarter of it off to be split eleven ways. On the upshot, and to their credit, there'd been little squawking about the division of funds from his crew. But this crew had been on around-the-clock call, weeks before the snatch of the rocket genius, Thomas Shaw. They were grateful, it seemed, just to have work, to get back in the game, overwhelming risk, poor pay and all.

Beyond the Turner's fever pitch for a rush job, there was a second problem, he thought, which was the FBI convention in the neighborhood.

Bowen, aka the Reaper, told his wheelman, Zervic, to park, then barked back into the cellular. "I'll call you when it's done. I understand." He heard he might be needed in Chicago for much the same disposal routine, so he was to stick close to the phone. The heat was on. If he could have reached through to the other side and throttled the guy...

Despite every scanner, radio and surveillance gadget available to black ops in scaled-down package in back of the van, he feared a ten-year-old kid with a fax modem and access to the Internet could plug in and triangulate their location. It would take a little more than that, he knew, but those exaggerated thoughts were urging him to end this conversation.

"I'll be in touch. We'll talk about it," he growled. "Let me take care of one fucking mess for you at a time." Hanging up, he said to no one in particular, "Guy probably still believes in Santa Claus and the tooth fairy."

"And Elvis is still alive," Cutler added.

"And the mother ship really did take Mulder," Stillwell said.

Some chuckles from behind his seat, but he knew they were all business. Dressed in black and completely harnessed, they were settling com-links in place, threading sound suppressors on HK MP-5 submachine guns.

A love tap or two on the slides of Glock .45ACPs, and the first round was chambered in side arms.

Down to business, good to go, he thought. The Reaper's Wild Bunch.

He checked the closed steel door to the target area. According to his local intel source who had already done the recon work, that would be the back service entrance. The problem now was he had virtually no idea how the interior unfolded. Another problem was the number of both combatants and noncombatants. In that regard, if it could walk, it was fair game. Scratch one headache then, since he had plenty of lead aspirin to spare.

It was seat of the pants, just the same, but it wouldn't be the first time he had to wing it when called upon by the shadow lords who wrapped themselves up in the holy shroud of national security. On the upside he knew some of the particulars on the DIA man's end of things, since he never went into any gig shooting deaf, dumb and blind. Since knowledge was power, he had spread a few items about the big play out in Oklahoma to a few of his men he could trust with absolute certainty. Guys who been down the black-ops road with him in some Third World hellhole and lived to chuckle out the war stories over beer and broads. He never went into a gig without a few juicy details to back him up, some extortion ace in the hole, just in case he was deemed expendable after cleaning up the other guy's mess.

Bowen took up his own HK subgun, fixed the sound suppressor. "One baseball each, gentlemen. Give me a flash-bang on top of mine. If we need more than that for this job, we won't be coming out." A sheet of inky black seemed to hang over the alley in both directions, nothing but shabby apartment complexes locked together or separated by service alleys for the garbagemen. They were all alone. Still, it was looking and feeling too easy.

Once the frags, plus one flash-stun, were handed out and clipped to webbing, Bowen addressed his crew, Zervic first. "We've seen the federal Ringling Brothers have come to town. Eyes wide open, Zervic. Battering Ram Two is in the vicinity. First glimpse we're going to have badges up our six, call them in and have them unload everything they've got."

"Aye, aye, skipper."

Bowen turned to the four men he would go through the door with. "Cutler. That golf ball ready?"

Cutler held up the glob of plastique, primed with detonator and cord. "Your razor's good to cut, boss."

"I go through first, standard high and low. Cutler, you're with me. I'm told these boys brought the harem, gentlemen, kids, too. All of it goes down. Let's rock."

And the Reaper was out the door, leading his black-clad wraithes across the alley. Time, he thought, to deliver a lesson in attitude readjustment. Just maybe, he hoped, as he closed on the door, this would go down, little fuss and muss. He hadn't gone over the details for his bonus fee on this job, but a clean sweep would go a long way toward brightening the rainbow of retirement he envisioned.

A river of blood first, a sea of cash later.

THE HARDMEN GOT it started with a bang. A swift shadow, advancing double time, and Bolan had the gap shaved to easy striking distance when the plastic explosive blew in the door on a clap of thunder. They were official-looking enough, com-links and HK MP-5 subguns fixed with sound suppressors, the whole unit moving as one with precision military bearing as they broke for the charge, two high, two low, one lagger to watch their six. Could have nearly passed themselves off as a legit SWAT unit, but Bolan suspected otherwise. Despite interagency rivalry with matching rhino-sized egos forever striving for the brass ring of the big collar, Bolan knew any official raid would have been brought to the attention of Broadwater's superiors.

In this case, silence on the official end was not golden.

This was a killing crew, and they were through the smoke and inside just as Bolan was bringing the Uzi to bear on the ghost assassins who had the drill down. The three *W*s—who, what and why—were shelved as the soldier marched ahead, scoping the van. He was thinking that with any luck at all he could bag a gunner or any mark fortunate to make it through the coming massacre when the van with all of the antennae appeared.

With the engine running, Bolan knew the crew had left behind the wheelman, maybe another gun or two in back to help hold down the fort in the alley. Smart money told the soldier their eyes and ears were on the horn, alerting the hitters that a threat of unknown origin had made the scene. The van was practically rocking now, the watcher agitated, no doubt, Bolan imagining the guy was a human pinball shooting around on his seat, one hand on the blower, another one grabbing up hardware to make a stand.

Combat radar blipping off the screen, Bolan anticipated what happened next. He was veering across the alley, going for temporary shelter from any storm behind the van, Uzi up and aimed at the doorway, when the trailing gunner popped up. The hardman was already in Bolan's full view, going for the easy tag, his muffled subgun slicing lines through the drifting smoke.

Bolan shot from the hip on the fly, the Uzi rising as held back on the trigger, and washed the fusillade around the doorway. Puffs of dark vapor took to the air, the shooter twitching in the doorway, absorbing hot lead. No Kevlar, then. The hardman was still fighting off the inevitable, grunting and flinging wild rounds that went skidding off the wall beyond Bolan. A few more 9 mm flesh shredders stuttered on, and the Executioner had the shooter waxed, limbs folding as the figure dropped in a crunch.

The wheelman jumped into the act next. Bolan glimpsed the van lurching as the driver dropped it into Reverse, going for instant roadkill. The soldier was out and running, angling up the side of the van for the killshot. Any slower on the break and Bolan knew he would have been bowled down, squashed. The Uzi chattered out long, angry volumes as Bolan's lead swarm imploded the window on the driver's face. He couldn't tell if he'd scored, but a dark cloud was ballooning up the hole he'd blown in, and the soldier kept grim hope alive. The van was swerving to starboard, then the aft slammed into the wall on a screech of metal and shattered glass.

The Executioner stepped up, Uzi spraying the windshield, right to left and back. The whole sheet came apart and blew lethal glass bits through the interior at gale force. He burned up the clip, hosing the interior, then stole a second to view the shattered ruins of the wheelman's skull, gray matter dribbling across the dashboard. Some sparks were jumping around in back, the snapping fireworks from behind the dead man telling the soldier he'd fairly gutted their communication and surveillance system.

Inside they were rocking and rolling beyond the battered doorway. It was a hellish racket of shouting, autofire and a thundering crunch of someone bent on bringing down the roof with a grenade.

The Lebanese taverna had just turned hotter than hell.

The first real danger, Bolan knew, slapping home a fresh 40-round clip into his Uzi, would be the charge in, running up on the rear of the blacksuited shooters without getting cut to ribbons before he fired the next round. Soon enough there would be more Feds, more blue and more SWAT barreling onto the battle zone. Throw in choppers, urban tanks, various departmental and precinct captains and commanders firing off their two cents over bullhorns....

This one, the Executioner suspected, was poised to rocket right off the ugly meter.

The tide of bellicosity rose in rock-concert decibels next when Broadwater's voice came booming over the soldier's tac radio.

"Belasko! Goddammit, Belasko, talk to me. Tell me that's not the sound of gunfire I hear. Tell me those aren't grenades I'm hearing."

Bolan threw himself against the wall, hugging close to his point of penetration. The bedlam was rising to new levels of fury, a babble of voices swelling the doorway, competing for the ceaseless roar of automatic weapons. The soldier knew he'd have to deal with

Broadwater sooner or later. Now was the worst of times, but Bolan unclipped the handheld.

"Stay put, Broadwater!"

"What?"

"Have our units seal off a perimeter. When the locals show up, flash your badge, grab someone by the scruff of his neck, whatever it takes. No one on our side is to crash this building."

"Are you nuts? I'm hearing World War III less than fifty feet from where I sit!"

"That's an order, Broadwater. I'm a little busy right now. Later."

"Whoa, wait a goddamn—"

It was a definite stretch to assume Broadwater could hold back the cavalry, much less sit on the sidelines while half the neighborhood threatened to get shot up to hell. In the heat of the moment, Bolan had neglected to mention that one of the home team was going inside. Should SWAT and whoever else came barging into the firefight...

Well, Bolan could only hope for the best as far as not ending up a friendly casualty.

No time to ponder what might happen.

The soldier went low, scoping out the way in. Muzzle-flashes were winking like Christmas lights, shadows wanting to come into view but the corridor angled to the right. The way in was wide enough, and Bolan heard the new round of howling, bodies thudding next, the dead, no doubt, already stacking up somewhere ahead.

The Executioner drew a deep breath, let it go, then surged around the corner, charging full bore into the slaughterhouse.

6

They were in and moving hard, a thundering juggernaut, and Bowen was itching to get the good times rolling. There was no such thing as overkill in the Reaper's unwritten tactical manual. The sight of blood, and lots of it, always got the juices running. The length of his body, scalp to toes, was feeling like one giant overheated radiator set to blow when the killing started.

The usual high.

They went for the gusto right off, not missing a beat, rounding the corner and hitting the first five Iraqis with extended raking bursts of autofire as soon as the jihad troops started barging out the doors to what Bowen guessed was their version of a war room. The first wave was ventilated to human sieves, lead dropping them hard, when the Reaper saw they were quickly getting their act together, grabbing up an international hodgepodge of weapons, swarthy guys streaming for the stockpile in the corner, howling in their native tongue. Everything from Uzis to AK-47s, Glocks to Makarovs, Spectre subguns and Ingrams were coming into play.

"Frag 'em!"

Three grenades aided the Reaper and his Wild Bunch. The bodies of their first victims had been pounded to the floor where the swing doors led to the kitchen, blood running like burst faucets thanks to the slice-and-dice treatment. It was mighty kind of them, Bowen thought, to fall so they could keep the doors wedged open, allowing him an easy toss. Frag one was armed and sailing into the kitchen as a group of five came streaming into view near a long stainless-steel counter used for food prepping. They were ducking autofire when the blast went off in their faces.

They were hell-bent on going down with the house, jihad troops bouncing off each other, holding back on triggers, bellowing out the rage, spraying and praying. They came close. Bowen was flinching as scorching lead went stinging over his scalp. Two more frag explosions tore through the war room, the shrieking of men getting shredded by countless lethal steel bits like classic rock to his ears.

An arm, sheared off at the shoulder, came whirling out of the smoke, skidding past Bowen's position at the corner. There was pounding of feet from some point above. That would be the families of some of the jihad boys, women and kids, crying out in panic, stampeding around the second floor, wondering what was happening. At best, they would provide human armor on the way out. Either way, he knew they were marked for permanent deportation.

Then it turned even dicier, the world about to fall apart, his instincts having already warned him it had been too easy, too quiet on the way in. And Bowen heard Zervic alerting them to an intruder coming for their rear. A big dark guy with an Uzi subgun. It didn't quite sound like standard FBI hardware to him, but it was another headache to deal with, just the same. He kept hugging the corner, catching sight of more Iraqis breaking through the kitchen, triggering weapons on the fly. It cost him a critical second, bullets whizzing all around, drumming the wall, but Bowen got his bearings, saw that the hallway they'd secured as a firepoint led out to the dining room. If they gained access to the dining area, and now with an unknown hostile—or even a pla-toon of Feds storming the place—they'd be hemmed in, soon to be chopped up into dog meat.

Bowen barked out the order for Stillwell to fall back and take care of their mystery guest. Bullets were snap-ping the air around Reaper and crew like a buzzing swarm of wasps, rounds gouging furrows through the wood paneling, missing their scalps by millimeters. He signaled for Cutler and Simmons to move out for the dining room, gave the order for another round of frags. That left him and Tyler to nail it down in the war room.

Cutler and Simmons hauled it for the short run lead-ing to the dining area, firing in unison as they made the far corner, one high, one low.

Teamwork.

Bowen went back to work, hit the kitchen with a long stream of 9 mm lead, scored another jihad flunky, sent him crashing through pots and pans while the storm chased the runners toward the dining room to get a lead greeting by his troops down there. A fresh magazine slapped home, cocked and locked, he was rolling for the smoke cloud when he suddenly discovered he was alone. Glancing over his shoulder he saw Tyler pitch-

ing to the floor, the back of his skull blown off. The direction of the killshot told Bowen he was in all likeli-
hood down two more men beyond Tyler.

Mr. Uzi was on the march, he knew, coming to join
the fun and games.

IT WOULD PROVE a colossal waste, a sorry and unseemly
death of the jihad dream, if they all went down under
the FBI guns. Mahlid wasn't about to see all the blood,
sweat and toil go down the toilet simply because he'd
neglected to post a few lookouts. Part of the failure was
certainly his to bear, but there was no time for regret,
any degree of mental self-flagellation that might cost
him more than a place of business. Either way, the
restaurant was finished, and they were bailing.

Which looked a definite reach for the stars at the
moment, considering the amount of ass getting kicked
by their mystery invaders.

Whatever was happening, it was all the sound and
fury of hell unleashed, and none of it was good. The
enemy had blown the back door, sounding the alarm to
get them jumping to their feet and grabbing up the hardware. Four, maybe five of his men had bulled out the
door of the war room, perhaps pumped by his steely
words of wisdom moments earlier, only to go down in
the opening rounds. These killing sweeps were so long
and overextended, the Iraqi leader knew something was
wrong with the black-garbed invaders. It was almost as
if they were killing his men with glee. For some reason,
the sound suppressors on their subguns didn't swell him
with much confidence, either. Then the grenades, something of a flagrant contradiction against sound-sup-

pressed subguns, started flying, and he knew these blacksuited marauders were not there to issue search warrants, raid the store for a clean lockdown, Miranda getting recited, chapter and verse.

This was an execution squad, plain and simple.

Quick feet saved his skin for the moment, as Mahlid saw the steel eggs flying into the room. It was foresight, more than anything else, when he had gone over the architectural layout with the Lebanese contractor. Plenty of offshooting hallways, antechambers, four doorway exits altogether, with a fire escape up top, near the end of the second floor. That didn't include windows in each of the four apartments, nor a stairwell that led to the roof. Tragic but true, his own family of six was the last concern on his plate of woes, since he didn't figure to see the next sunrise. Everybody was on their own. And if and when these executioners finished with the men, the women and children were sure to be next in line, a killing encore that would show them just as much mercy as the first casualties.

None.

The closet that had housed a fair bulk of weapons and explosives was in his sights. He went in, tumbling deeper into the hole when the pealing wrath of twin thunderballs rocked his world. Smoke came billowing into the cubbyhole like some cloud of doom, choking his senses, stinging his eyes with tears. There was plenty of screaming now, meaning whoever had survived the scything whirlwind of flying steel bits out there was reeling about, firing deaf and blind. Somehow, he needed a riposte, but he couldn't think of much else to do but stand, square his shoulders and weigh back into the bloody mix.

On the stagger, he got lucky, finding a discarded AK-47 near the edge of the stockroom. The stock and barrel were dinged and scarred by the blasts but otherwise it appeared in working order. He grabbed it up and began flaying the doorway where a blacksuited figure was crouched, hosing down his bloodied and blinded brothers-in-jihad. He was pitching them all over the room, blowing them back into the smoke. It was an unholy sight, nothing more than a glimpse of bodies and torn limbs strewed about, and Mahlid knew if he didn't turn the tide quickly he would be on his way, sans any chance of success for even a mini-jihad on the streets beyond. He hadn't come this far, risked so much, put his very family on the edge to not go all-out and try to save whatever he could to keep the dream alive.

He was moving to the side, firing on the run, and came up behind four of his men who were piling into a doorway that led past the kitchen to a hall, which in turn fanned out toward an exit. As luck, fate or the simple need to stay alive would have it, the foursome had snapped up subguns and assault rifles, pouches and duffel bags stuffed with ordnance. He took this as a sign from God that there was still hope not all of them would go down in senseless slaughter.

That the jihad could stay alive and well.

He barked out the orders, telling them to leave the building. "If there are police out there, kill them on sight. Shoot for their heads. Grenades, whatever it takes. Run! Hide awhile if you must, but I command you to take to the streets. It is Allah's will you are still alive. Take as many infidels with you where you find them. Go!"

And they went, Mahlid pivoting, spotting a body slumped against the wall. He plucked three spare clips from the waistband and sprayed the war room as the invader swung his subgun around the corner.

He held his ground, willing the shooter to show himself. If necessary, he owed it to the dream to sacrifice his own life, if only to see a few of his men made it out of there to turn Brooklyn into something that would make Beirut look like a walk in the park by comparison.

THREE ENEMY KILLS. The Executioner was in and surging down the hall, another couple of frag blasts having just thrown more sense-cleaving racket into the fray, when he nailed the third blacksuit with a burst to the back of the skull, nearly taking the shooter's head off at the neck. That left three marauders. But how many terrorists under the roof? And then there were families upstairs, no doubt moments away from getting burned down in the cross fire, either shot for the hell of it or as part of the standing order....

Or snapped up as human shields.

Bolan was low, Uzi leading his advance, eyes wide open for any sudden grenades bounding his way. If the killing crew had called in backup, how many more shooters could he expect to come crashing in?

The soldier knew he had his hands full, whatever form of cavalry broke the perimeter and wanted to join the slaughter circus. They were shooting up the house from all points, it seemed, a din of reverberating autofire and the sharp cries of combatants getting gutted by hot lead. Two opposite firepoints sounded off. Long, angry bursts told him the frag bombs hadn't cleared any rooms of standing opposition altogether.

The Executioner took up position at the end of the hall, glimpsed a skeletal figure with a complexion gray as smoke, and lurched back. The guy was good. Bullets were flaying the edges of the corner, chasing the soldier for cover. Bolan considered a frag bomb, but checked his hand as he started to reach up. Staying penned down was the worst of possible worlds. Second worst might be using up a frag grenade on one hardman, just to get him closer to both warring parties, navigating some course of action where he could secure an unimpeded firepoint to create his own shooting gallery.

A few jihad troopers, snarling off to his side in Arabic, made the call for him. Coming low around the corner, Bolan was holding back on the Uzi's trigger, his tracking line nearly catching the first gunner in midflight before the man had flown over the stack of dead men and vanished into the kitchen. The gray marauder must have done all the damage he figured he could for the time being, Bolan glimpsing three, then four bloodied stick figures stumbling out of the smoke where the frag detonations had wiped out at least a dozen men in there for good, hard to tell since a few severed legs and arms were scattered here and there.

The Executioner saw they were focused on the black-suit, unaware at the moment he had joined the party. They were cursing in Arabic, directing autofire into the kitchen, hoping to catch him with a lucky burst, when Bolan pulled the pin on a steel egg and chucked it their way. In the process, he nearly got his arm blown off as some alert shooter from the other end poured it on, rounds slicing a hot slipstream over his forearm, tattooing the wall above Bolan and driving him back to cover.

HE DAMN NEAR BOUGHT it, sailing over the prep table headfirst, gun extended, as the bullets started. Bowen did a belly slide off the other side, tumbled to the floor, jumped up and got his bearings on the run for cover at the end of the raised stainless-steel window that separated the stoves from where the wait staff picked up the food. Jihad fanatics now turned to wounded rabid animals, a couple faces half-eaten off by shrapnel, had almost charged into the kitchen, going for broke, when the roaring fireball shredded them out of play.

Mr. Uzi.

Who the hell was that guy? Bowen wondered. That was no standard G-man issue or even a garden-variety SWAT shooter. Unless they changed their method of taking down the bad guys, he hadn't heard where lawmen came crashing through the door these days—not in a PC age where the lawyers and the ACLU were still looking to coddle thugs, out there displaying all manner of sympathy for even the devil. Unless the thrower was a tried and true pro.

And Bowen had caught sight enough of the big guy to know a seasoned war dog when he saw one. He didn't have to walk back outside for eyeball confirmation Stillwell and Zervic had been eighty-sixed. He didn't need to get bogged down, trading fire with their mystery guest, either, to know it wouldn't last all but a few seconds. That guy was a hitter, just wading right into the damn shooting gallery, as if he belonged there. Something about the eyes, the way he moved. Bowen found it hard to believe, having ranked himself and his crew right up there, but he was looking at a serious heavy hitter.

There looked and sounded to be plenty of jihad goons left to hold down the fort, shoot it out to the last man, as he saw at least eight swarthy ones had somehow secured a firepoint at what looked to be a server's station beyond the far end of the cook area. Bowen also knew a few runners were beating a hasty exit down some adjacent corridor attached to the war room. One guy was still somewhere beyond the wall now, Bowen having already traded fire with the guy before he sensed Mr. Uzi about to boil up on his six. He stole a few moments to call in the cavalry, patching through to Battering Ram Two.

"We've got some problems here, gentlemen. Move in, but keep our wheels parked precisely three blocks north. Barnes and Crafton, stick with the wheels. The rest of you move in and give us a hand. Bring the heavy equipment and don't hesitate to light up a squad car or two. It's our asses or theirs. No exceptions."

They copied, and he was signing off when the lead starting hammering the counter above, a pan the size of a basketball falling and banging off his head. Reaper was cursing, the very notion some chef's frying pan nearly cost him his life, getting him in gear. It was the guy from the war room, coming through another entrance, firing his AK-47 as if there were no tomorrow.

There was little doubt in Bowen's mind that for a lot of guys under the roof, and maybe even outside, tomorrow would never arrive.

But Bowen wasn't ready to leave. He found himself itching for another stab at Mr. Uzi.

7

The Executioner rode out the blast, senses spiked by shock waves. The roaring detonation swelled the air with agonizing pressure to his eardrums, the ground and wall shimmying as he held on, counting on the grenade to make short work of more enemy numbers. The smoke and cordite blew past his cover. In no way, shape or form was Bolan looking to aid and assist the leader and his men of the killing crew—they were right up there on his list of guys to wax—but any gunman under the roof now was fair game, and any shaving down of prowling shooters was a fat plus, no matter how the soldier achieved a quick body count for the win column.

It was only a matter of seconds, half a minute or so, tops, since storming in behind the unknown marauders, laying waste to whatever lurched up in his face right off, but Bolan knew he was on the clock. The last thing he wanted or needed was for a bunch of SWAT heroes and NYPD's finest to come barreling into this apocalyptic cross fire. They didn't know the score, maybe wouldn't even care that a heavily armed bulldog on the home team was also inside, helping make Brooklyn a kinder, gentler place for its law-abiding citizens.

The Executioner was up, over and braced against the opposite wall, senses stung by all the blood, guts and other leaking body matter, going low around the corner when the shooting took on new dimensions of sound and fury. And the hardmen at the other end were gone— then he spotted the enemy blacksuits, leapfrogging over tables, vaulting boothes out in the main dining room, tossing around weapons fire to cover some new angle of attack.

The soldier gave his other flank a search. All clear but for the dead. Hearing became a definite problem all by itself, the din of autofire diminished by the ringing in his ears. Near deafness leveled the playing field on all sides, but Bolan knew his own burning sights for targets and raw combat instinct would take over next.

The Executioner spotted a feral face, swathed in beard, framed by a nest of curly black hair, shooting up the kitchen with an assault rifle. The terrorist—and Bolan could well assume this slaughterhouse was nothing other than a once swarming hive of jihad fanatics planning some doomsday for the citizens of New York— was hosing down the kitchen with long bursts from his AK-47. He was going for the blacksuit leader, most likely, when Bolan decided to clean up any malingering threat on his rear, whether it was one or ten shooters. The Uzi up and locked on, he hit the trigger, stitching a quick burst across the shooter's chest, flinging him from sight.

Another one down, but how many left?

The Executioner charged on, the waves of autofire breaking through the ringing in his ears, urging him on as he hit the end of the corridor. They were going at it, nearly toe-to-toe, he found, flinging dozens of indiscriminate rounds all over the dining room. It was nothing short of a storm of flying glass and wood chips scything the air, all of it just another lethal rain from hell. Bolan saw the marauders firing again on the fly, threading quick, short dashes from table to table, pillar to pillar.

At the west wall a group of fanatics was pumping out the autofire from an assortment of subguns and assault rifles. Bolan knew he had secured dicey cover at best, his rear exposed to anything that might pop up from the smoke and ashes. The marauders appeared intent on cutting off the terrorists from making some charge for the front doors and gaining the street to flee the scene. Bolan took in the foyer, the running plate-glass window, the massive golden bull right where Broadwater claimed, looming up in the middle of the room like some pagan god from ancient Babylon.

Bolan noted several hopping points to gain a closer killing edge were staggered all over the joint. The other side of that double-edged sword was any shooter could hunker down, take this one way past any reasonable wrap-up point if he had enough clips.

The soldier knew he needed this nailed down quickly before the good guys bulled in, throwing still more gasoline onto an uncertain fire that was rapidly spreading out of control.

Bolan scoped out two, then three runners breaking from a pack near some expanded service station, computers and glass racks taking a hell of a pounding over there, gunners howling out the pain and surprise. Beyond that circle of sadistic thrashing, there was general pandemonium. The soldier made out the wailing of women from some point above the shooting mob, a couple heads turning, shouting something up the steps in Arabic.

Staying put was tantamount to a sure death sentence, so Bolan began firing on the marauders, drilling a few errant rounds up a pillar, chasing them to cover but alerting the blacksuit duo he was back in the game.

Breaking cover, the Executioner shifted his aim to the lunatic pack, holding back on the Uzi's trigger on the fly. He was bounding up a short flight of steps to a landing when two runners burst from the far end of the bar, racks of liquor bottles going off like minefields. If they were looking for some fighting withdrawal, one of the mystery blacksuits helped them achieve their goal. It was most certainly not quite what the terrorists had in mind, as they were shot on the dash, lifted off their feet and pitched through a plate-glass window.

"THANKS, GUY."

Whoever he was, Bowen knew the lone dinosaur wasn't thinking about saving anybody's skin but his own, while torquing up the killing heat on his end. The Reaper was now back in play. The jihad nut with the AK-47 had nearly bagged him, driving him into some narrow alcove between the end of the waiters' window and a small office cubicle. The line of Uzi autofire had followed up almost on the heels of the frag bomb, which had blown the swing doors to smoking matchsticks, bits and pieces now floating through another pall of smoke, fluttering to rest on more Iraqi bodies.

The Reaper scoured the kitchen, the smoking mouth where Mr. Uzi had decimated his batch of Iraqis, then focused on the shooting gallery just ahead.

All systems go, locked on again. He hit the trigger on his HK MP-5, catching one jihad trooper up the spine downrange before he sprayed the whole station, added more bedlam and terror to the whole churning bloody mix. They were shouting all around, whirling this way and that, shuffling away from his swarm of lead, when Bowen forged deeper across the kitchen.

This one, he knew, was a long way from getting wrapped, with the outcome every bit a fat mystery as his guest. He'd keep his eyes peeled, just the same, since every bit of battle instinct he owned told him the loner could rise out of nowhere, anytime. No more surprises, Bowen told himself, feeding his SMG a fresh clip as the magazine burned out.

It was time to go for the gusto once again.

MARCUS BROADWATER wasn't the sort to stand around, while the mother of all urban wars hit the fan, and right in his face. Inside the target building it was nothing short of full-scale war. The windows were lighting up with muzzle-flashes like some illegal indoors Fourth of July show. Fire hazard was the least of it, but some raging out-of-control blaze was sure to start soon enough. Beyond all the racket of autofire, he heard grenades thundering off, crunching blasts resounding every few moments or so. It was close-quarters slaughter in there, no doubt, since he made out the lancing cries of men getting cut to ribbons by bullets and bombs, a lucky—or unlucky—few carved up by all the flying steel whipping around after the frag blasts. Hell, this was something out of Bosnia, he had to imagine, or Beirut, even the West Bank these days. Not Brooklyn. There wasn't a cop or SWAT bunch in this town, he feared, who had the weaponary on hand to nip this kind of action in the bud.

Not a chance in hell.

But there it was, the world—or this pocket of it, at any rate—going up in raging warfare. If he hadn't seen it himself...

He was wondering how to proceed, since Belasko's standing order made it sound as if he was supposed to take five, grab a doughnut and some coffee, when the front window blasted out and two bodies slammed off the sidewalk. Broadwater hadn't spent fifteen years kicking down some doors along the way and being the first one to lead the charge himself to spectate now. He refused to relegate himself to some flunky role to simply file a boatload of after-action reports in triplicate when this storm finally blew over.

If it ever died down, much less sorted itself out. And sort out what? Beyond zipping the rubber up over a bunch of bodies...and then there were the women and kids upstairs...

Before he could give the mess any further speculation, Broadwater was out the Crown Vic's door. The agents under his and Belasko's command were squawking over the tac net, having heard all the commotion, wondering how the hell they were supposed to proceed. They had their orders, and he could almost sympathize with their stay-put-and-watch-the-store dilemma while the whole damn sky was falling around them. Almost, but his own problems, he was sure, were moments away from multiplying.

It was a faint noise at first, given all the hellfire threatening to bring down the roof of the taverna, but Broadwater made out the distant cry of sirens. He was moving for the trunk, watching the bodies heaped on the sidewalk, when another figure came flying out the gaping hole in the window. Broadwater had a good memory for detail, faces, and he recognized one of the waiters he'd questioned earlier. There was a big ugly assault rifle in his hands, a look in his eyes that warned Broadwater he was whacked out of his gourd on fear, adrenaline, the smell of blood or whatever. The M-16 was in the trunk, and Broadwater was marching hard, bent on arming himself for this special hellish occasion, when the gunman came bounding off the sidewalk, bringing the assault rifle up and aimed his direction, as if the bastard was looking for the first available body to mow down.

Broadwater had the moment pegged before the guy even wheeled his way, was already hauling out the .45-caliber Glock when the first few rounds chattered from the weapon. He felt the heat, flinching some as the lead shaved past his scalp, then reflex took over, his finger squeezing the trigger over and over. He didn't quite see the hits open the shooter's chest, the target jerking all over the place in some weird jig step.

The gunner was down, flopping around for a long moment, then went utterly still, the life leaking out of him in great red spurts, pooling in the gutter. He hadn't counted the shots, but Broadwater figured he'd pumped five or six big .45ACP rounds into the guy.

Now he was the one jacked up, eager to get in there

and kick some butt. Not only that, but Belasko was only one guy, and Broadwater knew he could use the help. He cursed next, however, holding his ground as he heard the sirens closing from what sounded like the north, Fulton or Bedford Avenue. Belasko needed him out there now, waving his arms around, holding back the cavalry. But why? A strong hunch told Broadwater this Belasko character was a lot more than just a federal badge. Unless he missed his guess, Broadwater was reading military, covert-issue even. Washington had sent up a one-man wrecking crew to lop off some bad-guy heads, no questions supposedly getting asked on his end of things. The FBI, he believed, were meant to serve as little more than garbagemen.

Broadwater keyed open the trunk and grabbed the M-16. Just in case it came spilling out into the street.

Okay, he figured, he'd play Belasko's game, flexing official weight, reining back the army of blue, the SWAT guys, whoever else wanted to crash this particular Devils party. When this was finished, he was thinking, if nothing else, he'd covered his end, and watched Belasko's back in the process. The guy owed him a few straight answers.

That was assuming, of course, Belasko even came back outside in one piece.

"GET UPSTAIRS! Stay in the rooms!"

Jamil Tabrak was forced to bellow out the demand again as Mahlid's family piled at the top of the back steps, his view taking in still more shadows heaping up near the group. Women and children, he saw, and his heart nearly shattered.

Something about this was so wrong, and what he was telling them to do...

They had been in flight, going for the same back exit to the northwest service alley he and the three other appointed jihad brothers were looking to flee through to take their war to the streets of New York. The terror was stark in their eyes, and for a brief moment Tabrak felt a boil of heated pity for them. They had been brought here from Iraq, smuggled in, part of the whole charade, but their role was quite different than that of being front-line martyrs. He supposed now, with the amount of shooting and explosions, all the dead bodies he'd left behind, that their fate would be much the same as the combatants.

Death would spare no one there, not even the smallest child.

"Jamil, we must go!"

He heard the sirens somewhere in the blocks beyond the service alley, but he knew the American police would soon circle the entire building. And they would storm inside, join the pitched battle. And what if they were captured? Their leader's order was clear, and it was divine. Capture was unthinkable. Flee the building and take the jihad to the streets. Find the infidels wherever they walked, rode on subways or buses or sat in restaurants. Kill them all, and let the Devil sort them out.

Tabrak lifted the AK-74, prepared to trigger a few rounds over their heads to get them unglued, send them on their way to hide and to hope. Tahira gave him a look, contempt, if he wasn't mistaken, then began tugging her children away, shoving them back down the hall.

Death sentence.

A part of him wanted to believe there was another way, that he could lead them out of there to safety. There was a degree of hope, even still. If the police came and managed to gain control of the building, then the families upstairs would perhaps simply be taken into custody.

Jabal, Ali and Mohammed were yelling at him, urging him to go. A wave of sorrow and—God help him, he thought—self-pity held him rooted for a moment. He had no family himself, his own wife and children murdered by one of the many bombs the Americans had dropped on Baghdad. He had all too willingly, gladly accepted to join the plan the North Koreans had engineered with Iraq. He had nothing left to lose, and even his own life had not meant much to him after the deaths of his family, beyond doing the bidding of their leader, killing Kurds, executing officers and whoever else the great leader believed was a threat to his rule. Soon enough, he believed he would join his family in heaven.

Now was not quite the time or place. There was a war left to drop, the wrath of God himself, on the infidels. Should he die there, then living for as long as he had after the horror of what had happened to his family...

It would be for nothing. It would mean nothing.

He hefted the large nylon bag, slipped an arm through the loop. "Listen to me," he said as he shouldered his way past them and threw open the exit door. "We split up. Ali and Mohammed, up this fire escape. Go roof to roof over the next apartments. Find a way somehow. We are the only four who will survive here. We must carry out the jihad. I suggest perhaps one of you remain in Brooklyn, while another makes his way to Manhattan."

"How?" Ali asked, nearly shouting as the roar of

weapons fire kept swelling the air around them. "There will be police everywhere!"

"Find a cabdriver, I don't know. Put a gun to his head and force him to take you to Manhattan. There will be more targets there."

He heard the sirens, so close now.

The AK-74 up, he burst out the door, feeling his brothers-in-jihad on his heels. Sure enough, a blue-and-white NYPD squad car was barreling down the service alley, going into a long slide now as the driver stood on the brakes. Two faces behind the windshield, he saw, lit up with anger and uncertainty at the sight of four guns, no doubt, aimed their way. Only one unit, as far as Tabrak could tell.

Jamil Tabrak stepped forward, bellowing, "Death to America!"

And cut loose with his assault rifle, blowing in the windshield on the startled faces of the policemen.

"BELASKO! Talk to me, dammit! I just need to know if you're still breathing. I got an all-points. I'm getting set to stare down a whole army of SWAT. Give me something to believe in."

The Executioner was under a renewed storm of flying lead, bullets eating up the banister of the partition separating his latest roost from the main dining area. He popped up, triggered a burst as the blacksuits kept charging, vectoring, it looked like, for the bar. Bolan knew he was fast running out of time to call the shots, and he needed Broadwater to hold back the cavalry, now more than ever.

Bolan palmed his tac radio. "I'm still in the picture, Broadwater."

"I just tagged one of them coming out the store."

Bolan had briefly caught sight of a third runner, the terrorist having just made his dash to freedom. Only the faintest crack of a pistol had carved its way from out on the sidewalk through the racket piercing the soldier's ears. He didn't see the body fall, but had heard the familiar stammer of an assault rifle, fearing the worst for a moment. No time to feel relief that Broadwater or one of his men hadn't been shot down. The shooting war had maybe only hit the fifty-yard line.

"Call your boss, whatever it takes, Broadwater, but do not let SWAT storm this place. I've got women and children, unscathed, I think."

"Understatement! I read you loud and clear. I'll do what I can."

"Make it happen. Later."

Bolan was up and searching for targets when the hiatus nearly cost him. Two more seconds on the blower and Bolan knew he would have never known what hit him.

The hardman was in the process of going for it, wheeling around a pillar, a grenade in hand. The soldier had to risk it, rising up a few inches over the railing to draw a bead, his Uzi stuttering. Downrange the red minigeysers were spurting from the gunner's chest, but the frag grenade was already in flight.

Bolan was up and racing from the point of impact when it seemed half the restaurant vanished in fire and thunder. He was launched off his feet, hurtled toward some distant black hole that was quickly swallowing him up.

8

It was time to bail. Little more than a keen grasp of the obvious, Bowen knew, but if he judged the wailing sirens right, the light show was moments away from turning into a cop convention, with SWAT and federal troops ready to bombard the joint from all points.

End game.

The skies were likewise about to swarm with NYPD choppers, as Glenndennon patched through, telling Bowen they had one set of hawkeyes vectoring in. Bowen needed to clean up the rear before he cleared out or even passed off the next round of orders. Backup was on the way, and that was enough. He could talk when he was able to walk without the opposition trying to drill him up into human Swiss cheese. If he heard Glenndennon right, they had just parked Ram Two in a weed-choked industrial lot at the far northwest end of the alley. His men were coming out of the lot now, lining up the chopper, waiting on the flyboys in blue to get within range for an easy dusting with M-203s. He copied, just to let Glenndennon and the troops know he was still in the picture. He'd get back to them with further orders.

The Reaper had some ideas how he was going to vanish into thin air, but it would require a fair amount of finagling his own guys, maneuvering them into position, words of encouragement most likely needed to keep their resolve steeled. Maybe the promise of a bonus for a job well done, cash dividends, of course, keeping hope alive. Quick feet and loads more of deadly precision shooting were called for from there on, not to mention a little good fortune to help pave the golden road out.

Still under fire by Iraqi opposition, the Reaper moved out deeper across the kitchen, away from the cook's cubbyhole, gained a better angle of fire on their back side. He sprayed the service station, advancing, zipping them with a hellstorm of 9 mm manglers. The SMG stuttered on, Bowen sweeping it back and forth, the overkill chopping them up to dancing sieves. The final three jihad goons went down, limbs flailing and grunts sounding more like the angry barking of attack dogs. It was how the doomed final opposition struck him anyway, enraged to the last bitter breath—God, these bastards were hard to kill. He noted the last of them had been chewed to bloody tatters by shrapnel already, having somehow managed to survive their initial fragging to get it this far, only to get smashed for good by his lead hammer. One of them was minus an eye, and another jihad shooter was missing half his face, bone exposed from scalp to jaw. Another was an amputee, nothing below the elbow of his left arm.

Their pain was over, bodies crashing through glass, bringing down racks and computers, and Bowen was left wondering if his own horror show was next.

It was over, or so it appeared, just him and Cutler, a

pack of noncombatants above on the second floor. He wasn't about to assume anything on the way out. There seemed to be hallways and offshoots all over, meaning a few jihad shooters could have secured the second floor for a suicide finale. He didn't think so...or maybe some enraged wife and mother would be up there and waiting with a meat cleaver.

What a sorry way to go that would be, he thought. Time to blow the joint, no matter what was up top. Simmons, he'd glimpsed, had dropped for the count a few heartbeats ago, sacrificing himself to pitch an explosive where their mystery guest had apparently accessed a firepoint on some sectioned-off raised area of the dining room to the far east. Another thunderclap threatened to bring down the roof over there. Probably the smoking section, and it was, indeed, he saw, smoking up there now. He wanted to mentally tab up the number of frags they'd used, figured they were empty now, save for his flash-stun. He was grateful the late Simmons had hung on to one bomb, just the same. The guy had probably missed the earlier command to blow the war room to hell due to all the weapons racket, or maybe he'd snagged another grenade for himself before....

Ancient history.

Bowen rolled out into the dining room, glancing up the stairs off to the side of the bar. "Cutler, close it up to me, but cover my play. I'm going up top to grab some body armor."

The Reaper was feeding his SMG a fresh clip when he sighted the figure rising from the smoke and ashes. One eyeful was all he got, Mr. Uzi maybe a little worse for wear, cut and dinged, but the mystery shooter was vaulting over a section of banister still intact, like some Olympic hurdle champ. He hit the floor standing, bulling ahead, firing away with his Israeli SMG.

Just who the hell was this runaway human freight train anyway? Bowen was starting to think he was looking at Mr. Eveready Battery Commando and the Terminator in one unstoppable, rampaging package.

Cutler was returning fire, not missing a beat, barely grabbing some cover of a pillar closest to the steps. The mystery shooter's bullets were pounding wood and glass around the service station as Bowen hit the steps. He took them two at a time, several rounds tattooing wood from somewhere to his side, focused next on all the commotion as he topped out, kids crying, voices of women hidden behind doors bleating out the terror, hoping the storm would pass them by.

Tough, and damn unlikely.

Bowen kicked open the first door he came to, barging inside, shouting curses. Two steps in, and he was forced to slash his SMG across the face of a dark damsel who rushed him with clawed hands like some lioness protecting her cubs. Not a second to spare, so Bowen snatched the nearest available kid—a good-sized teenage boy—manhandled him out into the hall.

"Cutler! Heads up!"

He saw Cutler's head poking up, midway down the stairs, his guy pouring out a blanket of autofire, and flung the kid over the edge of the steps. Cutler nearly missed his human shield, the kid flopping up at his feet on the topple, but checked his firing long enough to snap up the body armor.

Cutler didn't waste a second letting their mystery

shooter know the score. "I've got a hostage! Drop your weapon, big guy! It's all over but the crying, hero! We've got a whole floor of live ones!"

While Cutler bellowed out the riot act in between bouts of threats and cursing, Bowen charged back into the room. Maybe it was pride, but out of a dozen quaking selections, he chose the lioness for his own shield, fisting a chunk of hair and lifting her to her feet.

"Come to Papa, Mama!"

Arm locked around her throat, Bowen dragged her out into the hall.

"We're walking out of here, asshole. We see one SWAT goon or Fed, we start wasting the women and children. It's your call. It's their blood on your hands if we don't walk."

Cutler was now shimmying into view, snarling out the play, working his way in an awkward backpedal up the steps, the kid locked to his chest. Bowen was halfway down the hall, looking over his shoulder, spying what looked like a set of steps leading to the roof, when his shield came alive in his grasp, the wildcat thrashing around, nails like spikes swiping for his face. She came close, nearly taking out an eye, but Bowen flinched back, felt the swish of air from the near miss cross his nose. Enough. Wrong choice for armor. Cutler would have to hold on, buy him a few seconds, he decided. Bowen shoved the wildcat away, brought the SMG on-line, and hit her in the back with a short burst of subgun fire.

HE LANDED ON TOP of a table, his crashing weight bringing it down on top of him, offering protection from both ground zero and flying steel bits. No time to thank Lady Luck, Bolan kept on ticking. He was up and over the railing, landing with catlike grace and firing the Uzi on the charge, when a worst-case scenario went down on the second floor. They were taking hostages now, as Bolan saw the gunner grab a boy who had been tossed like a ball over the edge of the steps. While the guy stayed jacked up on the curse-and-threat routine, Bolan secured cover behind the golden bull. The sirens were piercing the interior now, Bolan glimpsing the light show strobing against the jagged teeth of shattered glass over his shoulder.

He let the Uzi hang low by his side, unleathered the Beretta and slowly stepped out from behind the bull. It was a risk he had to take, and one shot would be all he got. He watched the woman on the second floor struggle with her captor. The familiar release of a sound-suppressed SMG made the other gunner falter, look over his shoulder, his eyes going wide as if he expected the rounds to come tearing into him.

Bolan didn't let him down for the surprise.

The Executioner seized the opening, caressed the Beretta's trigger. The 9 mm round cored the hardman between the eyes, a red hole blossoming, framing stunned features just as the hardman had returned focus back to his immediate problem.

They were wailing like the damned from above now, feet stampeding the hall, voices shooting down the stairs in Arabic. There was hysterical crying and gnashing of teeth up top, but Bolan had to wade through it if he wanted to track down the leader. The soldier was giving the boy a safety check on the move, the kid up and stumbling back up the stairs, when an armed and bloody figure came staggering from the kitchen.

The hideous wheezing of a punctured lung was followed by a brief stutter of autofire. Bolan darted to the side as the 7.62 mm rounds sliced off the golden bull. The Beretta was up in a heartbeat, tracking on, and Bolan squeezed the trigger repeatedly on raw adrenaline. The terrorist he thought he'd nailed in the kitchen went down for good this time, his face obliterated in a crimson wash. The falling shooter held back on the trigger, unwilling to give it up, pitching, wild rounds slamming into the ceiling, shattering a bank of lights. Glass rained down on top of his twitching form.

Running, the Executioner stowed the Beretta, then bounded up the stairs. Uzi up and leading the way, he was braced for the leader to be on hand, even firing away as he topped out, maybe another human shield in tow. One look beyond the teeming mass of terrified women and children, and he knew the hardman had stolen enough time to make a run out of there. Up or down? Bolan wondered. He then saw he would be forced to deal with the mob, uncertain of what he read in their faces. Fear, for sure, but a few of the women looked set to tear into him with bared hands like talons. Understandable to some extent, since they had just been left widows, but on the other hand they most likely knew why their men had been slaughtered. Beyond the children, Bolan wouldn't count anyone under the roof as innocent.

Bolan told them, "Police! Get in your rooms and stay there. It's over. You'll be safe."

The Executioner was waving the Uzi around, repeating the order, shouldering his way through the mob. He spotted a dark-haired woman, on her knees beside a bloody figure, halfway down the hall. She was weeping, shaking the body as if that would somehow raise the woman from the dead. A wave of hot rage boiled up in Bolan. For whatever reason, the leader had mowed her down, the line of ragged holes telling Bolan he'd shot her in the back. The woman was letting him know about it, too. It was pointless asking her exactly where the gray butcher had gone, to the roof or out a ground-floor exit, since she was hysterical, her ranting indicating she held Bolan every bit as responsible for the woman's murder as the killer himself. He was past her, leaving her to it, a good portion of the mob melting back for the safety of their rooms.

The leader was the only thing on Bolan's mind. The blue squad was outside, standing on the brakes, rubber squealing, doors opening and slamming, with cop voices snarling over each other.

Bolan skidded at the end of the hall, the Uzi fanning both directions. Yet another set of steps to his left, going for the roof. The opposite direction, more stairs, descended for some point beyond the kitchen, leading, he guessed, to a service alley. He was in the process of deciding up or down, when he made out the rotor wash, closing down on the slaughterhouse.

Scratch the roof. The leader probably had it figured a ground run was his best option.

The Executioner, senses buzzing on combat overdrive, descended the stairs.

"LIGHT 'EM UP! Take the shot!"

In record time, Bowen was across the service alley, up two flights of fire escape when he heard the rotor wash, damn near falling on top of him. He was at the window now, keying his com-link and barking out the orders in between searching the alley for flying blue-and-whites and the mystery guest. The glass was wire reinforced, meant to keep out burglars, crack heads and other neighborhood persona non grata. One-handed, he triggered the HK subgun, punching in the window in chunks while keeping the line open to Glenndennon.

"I'm under fire in the service alley!" Bowen used the weapon as a battering ram, slapping out the jagged edges that didn't want to give after the blast. "Take out that bird and get your asses down here to give me a hand! Can't miss it! I've got one unit shot up!"

"Aye, aye!"

"If we clear the field here, gentlemen, there's a fat bonus in it for you. If I have to, it'll come out of my cut."

"On the way."

Incentive was tossed into the hopper, or so he hoped. Bowen heard them laying on the tread along Atlantic Avenue, the cop floor show about to snatch center stage. He was squeezing through the window when he saw the citizens creating a maze down the hall, bleating out the confusion and fear. At first look, they were immigrants of various nationalities, but this stretch of road was awash with foreigners, he knew. That could spell trouble if any of them were linked to the dead Iraqis he'd put behind.

"Police!" Bowen shouted, subgun out and ready to start shooting if they didn't clear a path. "Inside! Now! You have terrorists in your building!"

That got them moving, doors slamming, a few malingering civilians needing some barking to on the way before Bowen found his flight for the fire escape at the far end coming into sight. The ploy itself, he knew, was a long shot, but escape alone was right then nothing more than a roll of the dice. He needed only a few choice moves while his foursome took out the eyes in the sky, clear sailing back to the van. While they unwittingly blew by him and charged the service alley, he'd be on his way. Already he was putting together a story for Barnes and Crafton....

Which reminded him. He keyed his com-link and told his ride to stay put until they heard further.

Now, if Glenndennon and the others followed up, threw themselves into the mix, going for broke against cops—

Then the sky blew up, the force of the blast shaking the floor beneath him.

Home run. Sweet.

It galled him to some degree, sacrificing his own troops so he could live to fight or spend the cash reward another day. But what could he do? Escape was hardly guaranteed, even if those four served him like some winning jackpot lotto ticket. Once he hit the ground, he could well leap out of the frying pan, into the fire, forced into suicide by the cops. Beyond New York, there was still a job in Chicago, and the council needed him to keep breathing so he could kill again. But he had a few demands on that score before he headed out for the Windy City. One mess was mopped up—well, almost at any rate—but personal survival came first, last and only.

Looking out for number one.

At the end of the long run, he threw open the window. Subgun poised, he gave the narrow alley below a search, the light show on Atlantic Avenue now shining like high noon, thanks to all brilliant fireworks of the mother ship blown out of the sky, down for the crash landing. All clear.

He caught four shadows, hauling M-16/M-203 combos, flying past the corner's edge.

Outstanding.

His luck was holding.

"FBI! I'VE GOT a man inside!"

Broadwater was marching down the middle of the avenue, official credentials out, waving the works around. He couldn't even begin to count the blue-and-white units screaming onto the scene, rubber smoking as squad cars fanned out, lurching to a halt. A look the other way, same thing. Barricade, as he found more cops, more guns, more snarling faces popping into view, edged out. Weapons were aimed toward the restaurant, then he spotted a few guns pointed at him.

"FBI, goddammit! Hold your fire!"

Suddenly he was thinking they'd shoot him down, for one reason or another, some of it having to do with the battle zone they found, maybe a few of them wanting to believe he was on the wrong team, wrong color.

It happened.

In fact, someone was barking at him, "Drop the rifle! Put the weapon down!"

Not good. He realized he'd hauled out the M-16 next, glanced at it as if were some radioactive hot potato. If he read those looks right, they were a breath away from mowing him down.

Broadwater wasn't sure which way it would fall, but the boys in blue were holding their turf and their fire. He heard the chopper coming in next, filtering through the roaring in his ears. Broadwater was looking up, thinking a sniper was maybe perched in the doorway, homed in on him when—

The sky lit up, a flash of fire consuming the chopper, stem to stern.

A roiling mushroom cloud towered for the sky, signaled all the way, he imagined, to Jersey. What the hell? They—whoever they were—had just added another dimension to this holocaust, telling all of them—the law—they might as well spit into the wind if they even thought they stood a chance at turning the tide there.

And Broadwater stood frozen in disbelief, his eyeballs feeling as if they were swelling at the sight of the flaming skeleton, wreckage now raining down or ricocheting off the roof, cops ducking for cover. Then the whole ball of conflagration that was once an NYPD chopper seemed to float for the ground. The boys in blue saw it coming, and even Broadwater was wheeling, sprinting back for any cover the Crown Vic could offer. He was in the air, skidding on haunches over the engine hood, looking back when he saw the flaming shell bang into the roof's edge of an apartment complex, carom next off the building, winging down, sheared rotors going for decapitation. They were little more than darting stick figures down the street as cops hauled ass a moment before the wreckage squashed a few units to scrap.

TABRAK GRABBED the barrel as Jabal lifted the AK-74.
They had come this far, and he believed they had been
blessed by divine fate. Whoever the four men in black
were—and he was certain they were a backup execution
squad moving in to aid the other vipers in killing their
brethren—Tabrak had spotted them at the end of the
alley. They had been too busy lining up the launchers
fixed to their assault rifles, holding their position outside a fence that sectioned off an industrial park. So intent on blowing the police helicopter out of the sky,
they missed two shadows running their way. Or so he
clung to hope.

It was a snap decision, based solely on the need to
clear the area unmolested, and follow through with the
sacred duty appointed them by Mahlid. The stairwell
housing, leading to a steel door, beyond which he suspected was a boiler or maintenance room, was yet another gift from God, he thought. They were burrowed
deep now, hugging the wall. They had nearly cleared the
end of the next apartment complex, when Tabrak had
seized Jabal by the shoulder and practically slung him
down the steps. They waited, the explosions and shouts
of men in panic seeming to hover over their hiding hole.
Boots pounded, Tabrak holding his breath, not releas-
ing his hold on the AK-74 until he spied the four shadows running past the stairwell.

Jabal had fire in his eyes as he put his face close to
Tabrak. "There will be police on the way. One of us
must make it out of here. I will take care of the police,
but you must survive, keep running."

That Jabal, whom he'd known since a boy in Tikrit,

would sacrifice his life, so he could carry the holy war to the streets of Brooklyn...

Tabrak felt the lump in his throat, then fought off the moment of weakness and nodded. "Go with Allah, then."

"Go with Allah."

And they were climbing out of the hole, the butchers none the wiser as they ran on down the alley. They were going to do whatever they wanted to, and Tabrak wished them the worst. He stole a second to pray for their deaths.

9

Four more hell hounds of urban Armageddon were unleashed and on the way. Murderous contact was unavoidable, unless they bolted on, down the main alley, passing the cross-running service corridor between buildings, and charged into the slaughterhouse. Bolan had made the visual seconds after bursting out the service door next to kitchen when he'd gone hunting for the leader. Rounding the corner, he halted at the sight of them. He was sure the blacksuited foursome had likewise spotted him before he lurched back, taking up cover behind a Dumpster. The numbers, types of weapons and the gap between them on first sighting called for a change in tactics.

A fresh clip already fed to the Uzi, the Executioner was betting they were the reinforcements, summoned in by the leader, and they would pursue him as the odd man out before they moved on to do whatever it was they were told to do. Which was most likely burn down lawmen, secure some sort of fighting evacuation for their lord and master. The downed chopper, the noise of the tremendous explosion fresh in his ears, was confirmation enough to the soldier that they had been ordered in, backup with the heavy ordnance to help the leader and crew blast their way off the block. Bolan had their selection of hardware filed away, and it was a safe bet they were going after uniforms with badges. Four M-16s with attached M-203 combos, the rocket launchers with their 40 mm payloads that had blown the chopper out of the sky. Two of them also had LAW rocket launchers slung around their shoulders, armor-piercing HEAT rounds that would cut through a SWAT urban APC and decimate the troops before they knew what hit them. The nylon pouches bouncing around their chests were stuffed with grenades, he'd bet. Plenty of killing tools to keep Brooklyn rocking for some time to come.

Not after he'd taken it this far, Bolan determined. He was way overdue to wrap this up.

The Executioner mentally ticked off the meter on the next set of doomsday numbers, opting for a flash-stun grenade to greet them when he made out their approach. With the sense smasher armed, Bolan kept his back pressed to the Dumpster. He could almost reach out and touch the metal hearse that was the final resting place for two New York policemen, the windshield obliterated, blown in on their shocked faces.

He couldn't recall having heard any gunfire outside when he'd hit the second floor but he'd been tied up in a shooting war himself. Which left him wondering—if not the leader, then who? Now cops were dead, just the sort of tragic disaster he had wanted to avoid happening.

"Where did he go?"

"Move out!"

Bolan released the spoon, mentally gauged the distance to targets by memory and voice, and whipped his arm around the Dumpster's edge. It was a low toss, a miniature steel ball skimming the surface, as it bounced along. One look was all he snagged, Uzi up and ready to flame. But the Executioner glimpsed the stunner roll up right between the legs of the leading gunner who had skidded to a halt, the horror bulging in his eyes. It was way too late to save the family jewels. Flash-stuns, the soldier knew, were most effective in tight quarters where the punch and blinding light was trapped to carve the opposition's senses out of their bodies, render them deaf, dumb and blind, virtual walking dead. The space between the buildings was a tight fit, just the same, and Bolan squeezed his eyes shut, hands over his ears as he anticipated a crippling blow, close to maximum lethal. Light and thunder burst in sound and fury, a scream echoing out from the eye of the supernova.

The Executioner rose, wheeled around the Dumpster's edge and went to work, chopping them up where they reeled in the smoke.

Two of them started shooting blind, spraying the air, the 5.56 mm rounds ricocheting off the metal of the fire escape beyond Bolan. But it didn't matter. They were already getting nailed, the Executioner's extended burst marching across them, left to right. Two men were tumbling when numbers three and four caught the last of the 9 mm rounds tearing into their flesh. When they were stretched out, Bolan took a step forward, thinking one of them was still breathing. Closing, he was sure of it, as the third gunman choked on blood, limbs thrashing.

"Bowen...bastard..."

The Executioner's senses felt pummeled by all the sirens and shouts of confusion and panic hitting his back from the street. He focused on the dying hardman, his fading gaze searching him out. Bolan thought the man was clinging to life, eager to tell him something.

"Bailed...sent us...right to you..."

With his eyes roving for any sign of danger, Uzi cradled, Bolan filed away the name. He could imagine what had gone down. The leader, aka Bowen, had called out the SOS, duped the troops into thinking he needed help for his fighting withdrawal. Too late, they realized they were nothing more than pawns.

"Rocket men...missile brains...they have one...."

A part of Bolan wanted to believe the man was delirious, lapsing into shock from loss of blood. Something in the eyes, though, the voice had just enough ring of sincerity to it, as if the dying gunner was trying to tell him something that might open an avenue for his own revenge beyond the grave.

"Three more...rocket men."

BOWEN WAS TREATED to the evil eye when he hopped into the van's shotgun seat. He was wound tight enough, having made it back. And that was a harrowing chore, listening on the run as what sounded like an all-units call from all five boroughs came screaming onto Atlantic, the whole siren show making it next to impossible to think. The last thing he needed was the looks now, but he was braced and armed with answers, just the same, for the obligatory round of questions, fired off in anger and more than a little suspicion.

"Where are the others?" Crafton, the wheelman, demanded.

"What the hell happened back there, Captain?" Barnes nearly barked in his ear from behind the seat.

"Cops, that's what happened. They're dead, all of them."

He caught them exchanging a look. Unconvinced.

"You want to drive us out of here, Crafton? Or maybe you want to go back and hope New York's finest is in a listening mood?"

Crafton looked set to pound the wheel, the storm building in his eyes. "Where to?"

"Take us to Queens." Bowen checked the street beyond the lot. Clear. There were enough side streets and residential neighborhoods but part of the problem was the city was just about to come awake, and the neighborhoods were sure to be up and watching now. "We'll take the Queensboro into Manhattan. Easy," he growled, as Crafton gave the engine some gas, looking set to give any NASCAR driver a run for his money just to put quick distance between them and the cop circus. "Nice and easy. We'll cut through Manhattan. Hey, I think the UN Building will be on the way. If one of you guys has to take a leak we'll stop and hang the lizards right there on the steps," he said, trying to lighten their mood, but the stony looks he received warned him they were short on more than just humor.

"Okay. We'll take the Lincoln Tunnel into Jersey. We need to hole up, a motel in Hoboken, Union City, something like that. Cool our heels. I need to make a call to our employer anyway, figure out the next move."

It was a good time to build a smoke screen, the end

of the line already mapped out in his head. "The short and the bitter—it hit the fan, gentlemen. The people who sent us neglected to mention a couple of items. Number of marks for starters. We must have left behind thirty dead Iraqis. We did our part, and I never like losing even one man. But somebody's math on the other end isn't computing. That also goes for the chump change they shelled out for us to nearly eat the worm there."

He couldn't be sure if they were buying it, since these guys were former black ops for the Company and NSA at one time or another. They could smell con job a mile off, keep it to themselves with a straight face until they decided to even the score. They weren't squawking, bombarding him with any more questions, so he wanted to take that as a sign he had put out the fire of suspicion for the moment. "Okay. Crafton, when we get in Jersey, stop at the first convenience store you see. I don't know about you guys, but I could sure use a cold beer."

ANOTHER TASTE of hell was waiting for Bolan as he cautiously moved out of the alley and onto the street. Uzi grasped in one hand, hung low by his leg in what he hoped was a nonthreatening gesture, the soldier was all fire and iron just the same. He was steeled for anything, but what he found—and feared next—was that whatever happened there was only a small dose of something far more monstrous lurking in the wings.

First thing after tagging the four hell hounds, Bolan had raised Agent Broadwater to tell him he was coming out, pass the word to NYPD. As anticipated, the Executioner now found more cops, more squad cars choking the avenue in both directions, their lights strobing the immediate sky above to form an illuminated halo. The air itself was a chokehold of burning fuel, roasting flesh and stinging cordite.

And the way out the alley was on fire.

The chopper's flaming carcass had crushed a couple blue-and-whites at the end of its plunge, the firestorm raging to his two o'clock. Fuel tanks were ignited in the blaze, and twisted metal went winging around, banging off residential or commercial abodes, glass shattering as storefront windows took a beating, burglar alarms touched off to add to the next round of hellish racket. By now, civilians were out in force everywhere, it seemed, mostly on the fringes or hanging out windows. Spectators, for the most part. Whatever cops could be spared were holding back the curious and frightened throngs. More distant sirens were screaming from somewhere, everywhere.

And the war wasn't quite finished.

The soldier found a small army of blue locked in a firefight with enemy unknown, a block or so west. Small-arms fire rattled the air, muted to some extent by a solitary voice of booming rage and the assault rifle barking from some distant point at the edge of an apartment complex. Bolan could have rushed down there, hurled himself into the mix, but the danger of getting dropped by understandable itchy trigger fingers by the home team became a grim reality if he made any sudden moves. Voices were already barking at Bolan, the expected bombardment of confused and angry questions hammering at him from several points, but the soldier clearly heard Broadwater.

"Hold your fire! Don't shoot! He's a Justice Department agent!" The FBI man was forced to grab a cop's arm as he made a sudden swing with a pistol toward Bolan. "He's with us, goddammit!"

A thunderclap sounded down the street, and all focus turned back to the shooting in that direction. A squad car was flipping on its side, two uniformed figures sailing out of the fireball. It was a suicide stand. The fanatic showed himself next, charging out of the shadows after dumping his grenade, the AK-47 sweeping the iron wall of blue. Lights and windows blew in storms of glass under the shooter's barrage, but it was over in the next few heartbeats. It was hard to tell, with all the shouting and cacophony of weapons fire blistering the air, but Bolan thought he heard a short burst of Arabic curses, divvied up with "Death to America!"

It took an extended salvo by the men in blue to drop him, the suicide charger doing his damnedest to try to bulldoze his way into the line of squad cars, jerking as the pistols cracked on, gutting him open, swelling him with hot lead. The fanatic got his death wish, finally toppling under the hail of bullets.

Broadwater started relaying orders to his other FBI agents, sent them on their way to follow through, then stole a few moments to discuss procedure, house-to-house searches and roadblocks and such with police.

And Bolan kept his long deliberate march toward Broadwater, who continued calming and reassuring the blue force that the soldier was one of them. The Executioner felt dozens of pairs of eyes drilling into him, watching him in some curious mix of awe, confusion and anger. If he read the faces right, the blue force was peering at him as if he was an abductee who had been whisked off into thin air, only to be plunged straight into the very bowels of hell, now reappearing out of the void itself to live to tell about it.

Bolan, of course, hardly saw himself as any hero of the hour, not by a long shot. And he could be sure, given the fact there were a few dead cops scattered about, no one was about to hand him the keys to the city. It was never about heroic antics anyway, he knew, grabbing the spotlight, stealing the thunder, whatever. It was duty, pure and simple, and he'd been there with tried and true skills to back him up, bulling into the fray to tackle a ferocious enemy who might have slaughtered scores of innocents had Bolan been somewhere else.

Fate, then? Right place, right time?

Whatever it was, Bolan was hardly about to break out the champagne and cigars. Cops were dead. Bad guys were on the run. He knew from experience to trust his gut. And the soldier felt his instincts just short of a wildfire burning up his gut. The leader was somewhere, beating an exit as fast and brazen as he could. Worse, what if more terrorists had slipped off into the dawn hour, using the one-man suicide stand to cover a vanishing act?

At the moment there was little Bolan could do, but he had some ideas on how to proceed. It might require pulling rank or getting Brognola to throw his weight around, but the soldier wasn't about to sit on the sidelines, getting his ear burned about what he'd done or what he had to do. All manner of threats from the field director would be hurled his way if he hung around with debriefings and irate grilling by desk jockeys and paper pushers on the next horizon for weeks to come.

No chance.

Judging by the swirl of official voices barking out orders to get units fanning out and seal a perimeter, he knew NYPD was in high gear to chase down any fanatic runners. Already cops were charging into adjoining apartment buildings, marching into alleys, hunting for gunmen. After—if and when any more fanatics were taken down in the immediate vicinity—there would be long rounds of calming citizen nerves and hours of questioning. Armored and subgun-wielding SWAT commandos, the Executioner noted, were right then disgorging from any number of urban APCs. Bolan left them to it, angling deeper across the street as Broadwater headed to intercept him, then pulled up short. There was a far-off look in the FBI agent's eyes, as if he were seeing a ghost or something. Clearly he couldn't believe Special Agent Belasko had walked away from this with little more than a few nicks and cuts. The official soldiers went on doing what they had to do, but all they'd find, Bolan knew, as they barged into the slaughterhouse, SMGs leading the charge, would be hysterical survivors and enough bodies to load up more meat wagons than the borough probably had budget allotment for this sort of gruesome haul.

The M-16 in Broadwater's hands lowered, then the thousand-yard-stare wandered to all the SWAT guys pouring into the charnel house. "How many meat wagons should our guys call in?"

"A bunch. Let's take a drive. We're through here."

To his credit, Broadwater pulled it together, didn't

read Bolan the riot act. They were splitting up at the rear of the Crown Vic, Bolan feeling the big FBI agent treating him to a long measuring from the other side. "A second, if you don't mind."

Bolan stood by the passenger door, waiting for Broadwater to vent or whatever he was going to do, as the frenzy of the official mop-up buzzed all around them. He'd already gathered a read on the situation unfolding. Cops and SWAT were scurrying around on all points, too busy for the moment to pay much attention to anything other than diving sifting through the madness and the wreckage as uniforms waved in the meat wagons, emergency medical vehicles and firetrucks, or holding back civilian throngs spilling out from other buildings. Bolan knew this was the best chance—or the worst time, depending on the point of view—to make a quick and quiet exit.

"You know, my career's probably going to get hung over the toilet bowl after this. I'm seeing the Director, hell, the mayor and I'm poised to flush it all, pension, benefits, the works. But you know something, Special Agent Belasko? For some strange reason, beyond taking care of my wife and kids, I don't care if they hang me out for the wolves. I'm looking at dead cops, guys with families like me, something that's not supposed to happen here. I'm looking at you, and I'm thinking but for the grace of God this could have been worse, only don't ask me how. My gut's talking to me, Belasko. It's telling me you're not some standard issue out of Wonderland. I figure you owe me, at best, a half-assed answer, since I kept the boys in blue from storming your rear or cutting you to ribbons on your walk out. So, what are you really?"

Bolan held the man's look across the way for a moment. "I'm a soldier."

Broadwater nodded. "And this is some kind of dirty war against terrorists bringing jihad to America?"

"Close enough."

"Suppose that's as much as I'm going to get for my trouble."

"It's the best I can do."

"Need-to-know, and all that?"

"Agent Broadwater, if you catch any flak about what happened here, the man who sent me will make a call to the right people on your behalf."

"Telling me you've got that kind of clout?"

Bolan didn't answer. He gave the slaughter zone one last scoping, felt the rage knotting a cold ball in his gut that a few good men had gone down for good. "Take a look around."

Broadwater did.

"I'm thinking there are a few murderous snakes that somehow slithered away. Pure murder and mayhem in their hearts. All it would take is one or two like the butcher on the F train. One pistol or subgun, a couple grenades..."

"This is just a preview? Of what? The coming attraction?"

Bolan couldn't be sure what the next hour would bring to the city. Beyond their own two-man roving sweep of the surrounding blocks—hunting for armed wanna-be martyrs, or the leader himself, while Broadwater tried to plug up the coming dam burst of rage from his superiors—the soldier needed to touch base with Brognola. And beyond dumping the bad news on the big

Fed's doorstep, the soldier would keep moving, searching, waiting for madmen to blow. Again he couldn't be positive there were a few human time bombs set to go off, but Bolan wasn't ready to close shop yet.

Bolan opened his door. "The main event, something like that, I'm afraid. I hope I'm wrong...but I'll spell it out for you best I can while we ride," the Executioner said, and climbed in with Uzi in hand.

The soldier was closing the door, but caught Broadwater falling back into jaded grumbling form. "Yeah, let's get the hell out of here before these guys start calling you Callahan, or Cobra, or something."

Broadwater was inside, took the wheel, dropped it into drive, and not a moment too soon. He was pulling away as Bolan spotted two uniforms rolling up, one of them calling out, "Hey! Where the hell you two going?"

10

Mohammed Khuban viewed the crack smoker and his fate as simply another door opened by God. He felt his heart hammering in his chest, pulse racing as he hugged the edge of the dirty brick wall. Ali was behind him, spying on the junkie sitting at the wheel of their ride to Paradise. They were close, but so far away from seizing a vehicle that would take them into the heart of Manhattan to fulfill their dream of jihad. Roughly fifteen feet to be exact before they were on the way.

Their AK-47s had been shoved in the nylon bags after the roof-to-roof flight from the embattled restaurant. They had climbed down the fire escape of the last building, farthest from the fighting, while police shot it out with unknown gunmen on Atlantic—presumably the same snakes who had blown the police helicopter out of the sky—but God had seen fit to bless the two of them with safe passage.

Beyond Atlantic Avenue, they made good speed and time, sticking to the deep shadows of alleyways, keeping off the main streets as he had them recorded to memory. Khuban believed they had moved on a northeasterly course, closing on either the Brooklyn or Manhattan Bridge. They searched for a cab to commandeer, along the way, as the sirens and the shooting faded behind them and the immediate danger of confronting police passed them by. No luck spotting a cab on duty.

The city was now coming alive, horns tooting around the neighborhood, the sun beginning to shed light over the jumble of redbrick tenements and empty lots. Driving would present a nerve-racking chore if the police had thrown up checkpoints, barricades, whatever else, short of citywide martial law with tanks and troops choking bridges and main streets. If they took it that far, they would have to deal with the possibility of unleashing jihad on the police. Neither one of them had bothered to count the number of banana clips, bound together in twos by duct tape, or the number of grenades in their respective bags. Judging by the weight alone, he knew they had enough to kill a slew of infidels on the streets before they themselves were martyred at the hands of the American police.

After searching the windows and fire escapes, he found they were alone with the crack smoker. In Khuban's heart and soul, the fire burned for jihad, the swelling heat from its core in his belly telling him it wasn't enough they'd made it this far. The blood of their slain brothers cried out for vengeance. Nothing short of wholesale slaughter in the teeming crowds of Manhattan was acceptable.

A search behind, the cross-joining intersecting alley clear, and Khuban told Ali, "Stay here. Bring the bags when it is done."

He took a 9 mm Makarov pistol from his bag, chambered a round, then stepped into the alley, stare fixed on the black Oldsmobile. The junkie, he saw, was too consumed keeping the flame from his lighter to the stem, inducing his own artificial Paradise, a smoke cloud thick enough to gag a mere passerby roiling out the window. Something inflamed a righteous fury inside Khuban at the sight of this American, sitting there, openly defying the law with such brazenness and contempt. He realized how much he despised the country, its people. They were so rich and privileged in a land with its legions of unclean souls, he thought, they could afford to squander vast sums of money on poison, ruining their minds, condemning their souls in the process, even shredding apart their own families without so much as a care to the consequence on others with such sinful behavior. How much they threw away on drugs in this country he couldn't say in a precise dollar figure, but he suspected it had to be enough to feed the starving the world over. All the hope for a better tomorrow so many took for granted. The money they wasted on such foolishness, he decided, was the same as stealing from those who truly needed and deserved it most.

Had not the Korean colonel warned all of them they would bear witness at some point to such despicable weakness, such abominable lusts for demonic pleasures?

At around ten feet and closing he broke into a sprint as the junkie cried out in alarm. Khuban was bringing the Makarov up as the junkie tossed away the stem and lighter and keyed the ignition. His habit cost him his life, but Khuban saw this as something of an act of revenge, cleansing the earth of more sin, eradicating any future misery the man's behavior might wreak on the lives of people connected to him. He pumped two 9 mm rounds through the open window, into his skull. Blood and bits of flesh speckled the windshield, enraging Khuban for a moment over the mess as he threw open the door. Ali was already running with the bags, giving their surroundings a wild-eyed search. Whether the killing was seen or not, Khuban didn't care. He would be content to end it there, if necessary, shooting it out with the police.

He reached in, hauled up the corpse and dumped the body on the alley floor. The junkie, he saw, had three cans of beer left in a six pack. Khuban took a can, shook it, popped it open and directed a foamy geyser to wash some of the muck and gore off the windshield. He jumped in, took the wheel as Ali claimed the passenger seat.

"Where?"

Khuban eased the transmission into Drive. "If Allah wills it, I believe I can find the Rockefeller Center."

THE ACT, from start to finish, was rehearsed, down to individual pat moves and abbreviated dialogue, with the right dosage of heat and determination scripted and hashed over in his mind during the drive to Hoboken. First Bowen had the living to take care of, then act two, the call to Mr. DIA in Oklahoma.

As the first one into the motel room, Bowen claimed a bottle of Miller Lite from the twelve pack, then bummed a cigarette from Barnes, lit up, popped open his beer. "Help yourselves, gentlemen. Hour, two tops, then we're on the road. Turn on the tube, see if we made the news." Actually he knew it would only take ten or fifteen minutes to do the deed. They had the end unit, the walls were built of cinder block, good to muffle noise. Beyond the door, chained and bolted by Crafton, with the man giving the lot and the industrial park the obligatory paranoid sweep by cracking the curtain, Bowen was thinking ahead. Since his description had probably been passed around, meaning APBs from there to Shanghai, he'd ordered Crafton to take care of the cash transaction with the desk clerk. Bowen managed his own bellhop duties, handling the duffel bag, with a cell phone with secured line and a sound suppressor inside, setting it now on the floor on the blind side of the second twin bed closest to the bathroom. They were near enough to Kennedy Boulevard, with bailing options from there to either Newark International or I-78. A flight to O'Hare sounded like the wise choice.

Moves first, then the big play.

The television came alive instantly with a female reporter on the scene of the urban battle zone. Bowen smoked, listened for a moment, unzipping the duffel while Barnes and Crafton worked on their beers. The reporter stated she didn't know much at the present, fulfilling her own role as the shocked and horrified messenger of tragedy, speculating next it had something to do with the massacre on the F train and terrorists. FBI was on the scene, as was SWAT, and so on, but nobody official was talking to her.

Bowen drained his beer in one gulp, flipped the empty on the bed. Cigarette perched on his lip, he reached down in the duffel, looking over his shoulder. Crafton was taking a seat in a chair near the radiator, with Barnes doing a slow step back toward the other bed.

"Not too loud, gentlemen, I'm making the call of our lives. Securing the future, you understand. Further orders from the top, but I'm going to make sure our friends understand they need to open the bank first. Way I see it, we've earned a bonus."

Neutral looks aimed his way, and he sensed their suspicion reaching critical mass, narrow gazes telling him they were chewing over the Brooklyn scenario, wondering. They were armed with Glocks, like himself, the weapons tucked in away in shoulder rigging beneath windbreakers.

Again something dark and smoldering in their eyes as they looked at him.

"You know, I've been thinking," Barnes said, reclaiming his perch on the edge of the bed.

"Yeah. What's that?" A quick delve, hunched, hands out of view, and he slipped the sound suppressor in the left pocket of the windbreaker, watching them out of the corner of his eye. He took the cell phone next, making sure they saw it as he stood, body angled to keep the bulge of the suppressor hidden.

"The time frame."

"Yeah? What about it? Keep talking," Bowen said, moving into the bathroom, easing the door three-quarters shut and setting the cell phone on the toilet's tank.

"The minute the hawkeyes went down, the others were headed your way. On your strict order. You were under fire, you said."

"Then you called us. 'Stay put,' you said."

"And?"

He kept his ears tuned in, envisioned them still on the other side of the room, looking at each other, working up the courage to get to the punch line. An extended silence he didn't trust followed, as if they were listening to make sure he was taking care of his business.

He let the cigarette fall from his mouth. "You've got something to say, say it," Bowen called out, the smoke sizzling out as it hit water. "We're all *compadres* here." He flushed, stepped back, eyes on the mirror. He couldn't see their reflection—which meant they couldn't see him—but he could feel them, holding turf on the other side of the room.

"It all happened too quickly, Captain."

"What happened? I'm listening." He was all empathy now, just enough sincerity, not too aggressive in his concern, he thought. Nice. Holding them back, but he could feel the snow job melting. Quickly and noiselessly he retrieved the sound suppressor and Glock, threaded in two shakes.

Ready.

"Hey, one of you pop me another beer, if we're gonna sit around and commiserate and draft eulogies for our fallen comrades?"

Grabbing the door's edge, he heard the hiss as one of them unscrewed the cap on a brew. Seeing the gun in Bowen's hand they froze, aware way too late there was no chance to jump clear from getting clobbered. He begrudged them credit for trying, just the same, hands digging inside jackets, but Bowen was already out the door and squeezing the trigger.

He nailed Barnes first, drilling one .45 ACP round between his eyes. Crafton was up now, clearing his weapon when Bowen beat him to it, tapping the trigger to give the man a third eye matching Barnes's. They fell hard, Bowen wincing at the noise, the blood and gobs of brain matter splashing the door and wall as hollow-point rounds cored out the exit.

He listened to the silence for a moment, any hint the occupant in the adjoining room might be roused and scuffling about, wondering. Nothing. He checked the parking lot, watched the traffic sweeping past, then went and retrieved the cell phone. He punched in a series of numbers. Two rings, and the familiar gruff voice barked on.

"Yes?"

"It's me."

A pause, the man's mind no doubt scrambling for one of his patented mantras. "You got some pair on you calling me like this."

"Thanks. I appreciate the flattery."

"Yeah. I'm watching the results of your work now on CNN. What the hell happened out there? You want to tell me why it looks like you created just the sort of mess I wanted to avoid? You want to tell me why I—and our people—am deeply concerned you might become a TV star?"

The Reaper glanced at the bodies as he walked out of the bathroom. "Let's just say I had a few problems, but everything's under control."

"Is it?"

"You're watching too much TV. I suggest something light for your nerves. A soap or a game show. I like the one where the babes parade around in bikinis while the contestants bid on prizes."

"CNN's got all it wrong, is that it?"

"You're giving me way too much credit, Turner. I had

more than a little help from an unknown source with the urban renewal."

"I hear the needle on my bullshit meter making these funny little whining noises all of a sudden."

"Speaking of whining, anybody ever tell you that you worry too much?"

"I get paid to worry. Part of the unwritten job description."

Bowen chuckled, hoping he came across every bit as mean and insolent as he felt. "In my experience guys who go thrashing around, claiming the sky is falling, worrying all the time have this peculiar way of creating their own self-fulfilling prophecy of doom."

"Now you're a philosopher."

"No. Now I'm the man of the hour who's set to name his own price. That is if you still want Chicago cleaned up. If you do, here's my nonnegotiable fee, cowboy, so get your wallet out...."

HE WAS WEDGED between them, felt the heat emanate off the bodies of his wife and daughter, out of pure terror or something else—rage and shame—he couldn't be sure.

Hours ago—and how could Thomas Shaw accurately judge time?—his wife had spoken briefly to him, asking questions he couldn't answer before the voice with the Asian accent barked at her to shut up. Shaw knew his wife as well as he knew anyone, had endured on more than one justifiable occasion a tongue lashing, and he anticipated her flaring up with righteous indignation and fury, ready to fight. She had growled a few questions at their captor, demanding to know where they were being taken and why before he'd heard him scuffling a few steps toward them, the voice raising in clear threatening decibels, the man perhaps poised even to lash out with fists or worse.

Shaw had a good idea why this was happening, and he knew the danger was very real, and imminent. He might have lived on the cloistered fringes of the violence and subterfuge that came with the turf of classified work, but he'd heard more than a few stories of what the black operatives, those jealous guardians of high-tech Pandora's boxes, were capable of. Quietly he had implored his wife to do as she was asked, offering what sounded now like lame words of encouragement to stay strong, the promise that everything would be all right.

Just what could he do anyway, other than offer words of hope, meant to soothe nerves more than anything else? He was a scientist, pursuing what he believed was a course of peace his entire life, searching for that one giant leap across the Rubicon where his own hands would effectively neutralize the threat of nuclear war. He was a thinker, an idea man, not some warrior who could fearlessly charge into danger and spit on the face of death. Violence to him was an affront to human dignity. Yet there he was, searching, hoping for some way to strike back, justifying imagined scenes of harm befalling their captor, believing if he didn't do something...

He pushed extreme images of any number of possible dire fates to the darkest nooks of his mind.

Wherever they were going, whatever was going to happen, he felt a growing and shameful sense of utter helplessness he'd never known. He knew it would be too easy right then, with nothing but time and mounting anxiety on his hands, to sit there and wallow in self-pity, doubt, loathing that he wasn't up to physically fighting back. Assuming he even found the opportunity for an attack that would prove suicidal in the end, maybe even fatal for his wife and daughter.

Since the past night minutes had dragged by like hours, time suspended, all but irrelevant other than getting to their unknown destination. It was mind games now, a way to keep his thoughts occupied, off the fear. He tried to piece together events, but after the three of them were herded into the chopper, the hoods were tugged over their faces, their hands bound before them with plastic cuffs. It struck him as some ghoulish act of arrogance on the part of their captors, the hangman's hoods instead of mere blindfolds. They were morbid trophy pieces now, if only for their captors's amusement and gloating. Their blind degradation was something he had always only believed happened in Beirut or Baghdad or Bosnia, where shot-down fighter pilots or American diplomats or CIA agents were abducted off the street, paraded before the cameras, black hoods hiding their faces as if they were moments away from execution.

The tight cuffs began biting into his wrists not long after they were fastened, but fear of interrupted blood circulation became the least of his worries. He tried to measure time, just the same, thinking he could mentally gauge direction. A left here, right there, listening for identifiable sounds, church bells or airplanes taking off, like he'd seen kidnap victims do in the movies. As if he could somehow slip away at some point, unseen, call the police or the FBI from a pay phone, direct them to the spot for a daring rescue. Grim reality was far different than the trappings of fantasy. So he gave up dwelling on direction and time, dreams of lawmen crashing down to free them.

Now they were sitting in the back of what he suspected was a truck. He was seated on the hard floor, cold on his rear, metal most likely. The bed was covered, with just a brisk shaft of cold air seeping through some crack, but enough to drive a shiver through his bones. The way muffled sound from the road below echoed around them, he imagined they were in a U-Haul, maybe a horse trailer, though he didn't breathe the usual smells of hay or the lingering taint of removed animal waste. The constant vibrating of the wall against his back told him they were traveling fast, on open highway. All these details, he concluded, meant nothing. They were prisoners.

Despite himself, he began feeling a wave of regret building inside. If not for him, his family wouldn't be there, kidnap victims, hauled off by men of violence. It was his work, his life, that might cost him his wife and daughter. It was some consolation, at best, that Sara was missing. And what had become of her? Was she...even still alive? He could only pray that she was safe, and free. If it was him, his brain they wanted, which he suspected, then killing any member of his family would only incite him to rebel. Or would they execute his wife or daughter simply as a warning? Say Sara had contacted the police? What could she tell them? Not much. Some of them were foreigners, he had seen at the house, but all of them, he strongly suspected, were links in a running network of connections and contacts to the violent shadow world that had always existed just beyond his ivory tower.

He could feel himself spiraling down into depression every bit as black as the inside of the hood. The waiting. The fear of the unknown. The hoping. His mind wandered, searching for reason out of this horror. He had heard once, unable to recall the occasion, that at the moment of death the entire panorama of a human being's life flashed before his or her eyes. From cradle to grave, every moment, good, bad or neutral, came together in an instant, the blinding wink of a supernova of truth and mercy, the sum total of events during his or her life for the individual to behold and to judge on its merits. There, then gone, or so he'd heard, but branding in its wake the revelation of truth and meaning of one's existence, with all the sorrow and joy, love and hate, regret, failure and triumph, every thought and feeling and experience of that particular life...

Well, he certainly wasn't dead yet, but he saw—or maybe conjured up—entire passages of his own life in his mind's eye. It came next without warning, an intense desire to curse himself as he suddenly loathed the selfish pursuit of his dream, with ultimate achievement as the only worthy goal in his life.

He could see it all, or the parts most worth remembering, or least painful perhaps. The wedding day. The honeymoon in Hawaii, the joy of their love that was fresh and new and exciting as they charted the course for their future together. The birth of his daughters. Every Christmas. Every Thanksgiving. His father's funeral. He saw them next, clear as day in his mind—Rebecca, Patti and Sara—the perfect family unit, happy on the surface, the husband and father doing and saying all the right things at the right time. Everything in order, no fuss, no frills, no interruptions.

But the picture he formed came to him full of holes, and he now suspected why.

Oh, God, he heard his mind cry suddenly, a tortured, lonely voice echoing out from the darkest corner of his heart. They had been more like window dressing for the world at large than real, feeling human beings.

They said truth always set a man free, but he wasn't so sure. Truth was, they had loved him, without condition, accepting him for what he was—driven, ambitious and aloof from their own needs, dreams and hopes and aspirations—while he forged ahead, leaving each of them behind, trapped in their own islands of silent suffering just to be loved.

Even then he wasn't sure how to react to these feelings, but a small voice in the back of his mind was growing, stronger by the minute, the more he saw the loneliness of their lives, the frustration he had created through his own neglect. The voice told him if he had the will, there was a way to change it. But when? And how exactly? And would he ever get the chance to try to make it right? And how did a man make up for years of stubborn living one way, then suddenly turn around and tell the world he'd seen the light? It wasn't that Rebecca had felt unloved all these years, or hardly abandoned while he chased his dream of saving the world from Armageddon. Or had she? And his daughters? How did they see him? Did they, too, feel adrift, disconnected from the human race somehow because he'd never shown much more than a passing interest in their lives? Or was simply on hand when necessary to pass down a bit of stern fatherly advice? He couldn't help but wonder now if he had gone ahead and taken his work to the base, as the DOD had tried to persuade him, if this would have never happened.

It hit him then, the air leaving his lungs in a sudden rush, as if he'd been punched in the stomach. His colleagues. Oklahoma. It was inconceivable, but he had already been betrayed by Rodgers, an assumed name, he was sure, an operative ostensibly with the NSA who was supposed to guard the castle. What if one of his colleagues had likewise turned traitor? Was this some dark conspiracy, envelopes of cash changing hands in some back alley? Were the four of them, who were on the verge of creating the prototype missile laser net for a bona fide SDI satellite, been sold like some commodity to a foreign government? Had one of them turned on the rest?

"Dad?"

Beyond the obvious fear, he heard something else in Patti's voice. Something, he thought, he'd not given her over the years. It was awkward to move, but he reached over and folded his hands over hers, gave them a gentle squeeze. An anger he'd never before felt coursed through him at the touch of her cold, trembling flesh. The very notion she was being forced to endure this shame, ride out whatever the danger to its conclusion, filled him with the closest he'd ever come to rage, and a primal desire to strike back.

"I'm here, Patti. I'm right here." He wasn't sure quite what he heard in his voice, but it sounded new, and foreign to the way he normally spoke to her. New, and leaving him to wonder if he was on the verge of turning some corner he never saw until now. Even some crossing over to a point of no return, becoming what he hated most in his captors.

11

Bolan knew the clock was winding down in New York. The Executioner also knew Broadwater couldn't run interference with FBI brass much longer.

Enter Brognola.

The soldier led the FBI man into the safehouse. Broadwater checked out the Spartan accommodations, the shell-shock still hanging on his expression.

"I need to make a call. There's coffee in the kitchen."

"I'd ask you got something a little stronger, but I'm in deep enough as it stands," Broadwater said, moving for the couch, tac radio in hand.

Bolan felt empathy for the man's predicament. He was a soldier in his own right, and duty had called him into the fray, the man laying it on the line for Bolan, and beyond his own career considerations. Broadwater had children to feed and a wife who worried about him coming home every time he stepped out the door. And now the FBI hierarchy would want to pull the AWOL Broadwater up on the military equivalent of dereliction of duty, just for starters. It would take some heavy Brognola muscle to put things back on track, everything short of a presidential directive probably, but Bolan knew the storm would pass as far as Broadwater was concerned. The Justice man's wonder touch was equal to raising the dead.

Beyond any concern over his personal future, the soldier could sense Broadwater was disappointed their sweep of Brooklyn neighborhoods on the way to the safehouse was uneventful. Other than threading their way past other units arriving on the scene, no terrorists, no murderous blacksuits turned up. It was possible the last one had gone down in a hail of bullets right there on Atlantic Avenue, but unlikely. In all the chaos and confusion of battle, with the Brooklyn borough offering every nook and cranny by way of alleys, parks, sewers, and with bridges leading into Manhattan, with Queens just up the way...

The Stony Man warrior's gut told him they were out there, human sharks circling, the smell of blood in their noses.

The enemy wasn't finished.

He walked into the bedroom, closed the door and found the specific section of floorboard in the middle of the room. He bent and fingered the edge, pulled up the large cut-away piece. He dialed the first series of numbers on the lock, clicked in, then went through another set to disengage the acid tank meant for felonious or curious hands if they got that far.

The backup war bag came out first. He didn't know what waited in the early-morning hours, but Bolan would be prepared with the works either way. The aluminum briefcase with sat-link was out, settled on the dresser. He worked the combination from memory, opened up and punched in a long series of numbers, opting for speakercom instead of the headphones and throat mike.

It wasn't unusual to find Brognola in his office around the clock when a mission was on the burner. The big Fed came on right away, and Bolan cut to the chase, updating the Justice man on all fronts. As usual, Brognola always expected nightmare news and didn't belabor the headache of having to chainsaw through the red tape. He'd deal with the FBI, and Broadwater could count on getting nothing but a commendation.

That said, it was Brognola's turn.

Bolan was pacing, wondering exactly where to take it from there, when the big Fed dropped the bomb and froze him in his tracks.

HE WAS BREATHING way too hard, hyperventilating, Tabrak believed, his heart like a jackhammer, ready to blow a hole through his chest. Adrenaline? he wondered. Fear? What? Some voice he should have recognized as his own, but couldn't make out clearly, was shooting all manner of tortured questions through his head. Tabrak growled out loud, shook his head, trying to quiet the voice. What was wrong with him? This was his moment to shine, something he'd lived for most of his life.

He had a sacred duty to carry through, for Muslims everywhere, for himself, for God. And it didn't really matter that he was unfamiliar with Brooklyn beyond his own block. He figured he'd put enough distance from the battlefront.

Tabrak had moved hard and fast, using the shadows of alleys for concealment. The din of sirens had faded long ago, and when he nearly stumbled across a police car rounding a corner, he'd hidden in a Dumpster. So why was he so afraid? He was still alive and on the move. Was he scared of dying? Was he questioning the mercy and the wisdom of God? Surely what he was about to do was right in the eyes of God?

He was on Seventh Avenue, breathing hard, catching strange looks now from passing infidels. He looked from the street sign to what appeared a commercial area coming awake in the early-morning hour as commuters and pedestrians began swelling the sidewalks.

Numbers. Targets. Plenty of potential, right there, he decided. What little he knew from war plans about this area of Brooklyn, mapped out by Mahlid, there were subway stops somewhere in the vicinity of Grand Army Plaza. Scratch the subway, he decided, shouldering his way through a couple, ignoring the brief outburst behind, forging down the walk. After yesterday, police were sure to be stationed on every subway platform, every car maybe. He told himself someplace where they gathered in decent-sized groups at this hour, somewhere with walls, few exits. A diner, then. Go straight through the door, the AK-74 coming out of the bag, grenades shoved in his pants pocket before he went to give them a final wake-up. Two clips were wound together, to be reversed with next to no lost precious time. Figure sixty rounds to get it started, more wrapped twin clips in the bag.

He was searching the street when the decision was made. He wasn't sure why the two policemen were boring dark stares through him, but the North Korean had warned them all their lawmen operated on something called profiling. Essentially, he recalled from one of the many briefings, they only needed to believe someone looked suspicious, fell into a stereotyped outline that gave them a right to stop, question, even search "the type." Mostly, he remembered the North Korean tell him, they were members of an ethnic minority, deemed shady looking on the spot, not belonging where the police thought they should belong.

Tabrak figured he must have fit the profile of what a bad guy looked like to them. He fit the whole bill.

Tabrak couldn't stand the struggle for air any longer, thinking his brain was about to shut down from lack of oxygen. The bag was already open, allowing him an easy draw of the AK-74. He laughed at the shock etching their faces. His breathing slowed, natural now for some reason, the voice of torment vanishing from his thoughts, as the patrol car lurched into a sliding halt near the curb. Tabrak swung the assault rifle up, held back on the trigger and blasted in the windshield.

"ROCKET MEN. That's what he said," Bolan stated.

"Became Judas on his deathbed," Brognola responded.

"It can happen."

"Dump on me, will you? I'll get the last laugh. Okay. I've got my own people, Striker, already at the Shaw residence."

"Don't expect the phone to ring."

"I'm not holding my breath for any ransom demand on this. My guys are staying put in Middleburg, both for the daughter's protection and to try to keep her calm. No media, so far, but I can almost see them licking their chops."

"She's sure they were Asian?"

"Positive. Bright girl, lucky, too, or somebody was watching over her, who can say. She's hanging in there, worried as hell naturally, I understand, but she's showing guts, considering her parents and sister were abducted at gunpoint right under their roof. The body left behind belongs to a branch of DOD black-ops security. My people found the whole security system, alarm, cameras, the works, shut down when they got there. According to Sara Shaw, only two people there had the access code to do that particular trick. And I don't think her father would have turned it off. The daughter says he was as security conscious as they get."

"Inside job. And they're cleaning up as they go."

"I know that voice all too well. I'm way ahead of you, Striker."

Bolan had no doubt they were on the same page. Questions hanging still, but the Executioner could be sure both Brognola and the cyber team at the Farm, led by Aaron Kurtzman, had done the usual digging, getting answers as fast and best they could to start piecing together the shrapnel on this puzzle.

"Here's where it stands," Brognola said. "Initial satellite imagery is showing me what looks like a spook convention in this little slice of Oklahoma prairie we touched on. U.S. government property, something like four to five square miles recently snapped up by DOD. The Army Corps of Engineers built this particular spook central.

"The rocket men are called the Titan Four. DOD, or whoever is actually running the show out there, has the civilian workforce, whatever spook or military personnel likewise housed on the base. There's a ranch house the Farm has put under the microscope. It sits all by its lonesome, a mile and change north of the compound, with plenty of vehicles, some with government tags, some luxury wheels, like they've got high-profile out-of-town guests. It has satellite dishes and armed sentries—I'm thinking black-ops central. Where the real shadows dwell. This is a classified project, involving SDI technology. Not quite a black project, meaning it would be buried so deep or floating out there in cyber limbo that not even our people would find the first glimmer of dark light.

"Striker, I don't know how they plan to pull it if off, but I know you're with me thinking this is a well-planned and well-financed conspiracy. I'm thinking it's going to hit the fan out there, a straight snatch of missile geniuses, I understand from Kurtzman, who can calibrate a guidance system on anything armed and built to fly."

"They're that good?"

"Number one. Gold-medal talent."

"It's going to happen, Hal. I hope I'm wrong, but I don't think I am. It's wanting to come together, has been since yesterday. Hell of a thing to point out, but we might have never gotten it this far, still in the dark, if the opposition didn't start eating their own."

"Because of the F train they had liabilities. One of their jihad recruits jumped the gun on the master plan, which was a massive terrorist strike. I'm thinking they covered their exit, or used it as a threat to unload on American citizens while they hauled the Titan Four out of the country."

"That would be my guess." The Executioner relayed his suspicions about Chicago, while Brognola stated he'd put the FBI and Justice on alert across the nation. "We've been down this classified road to hell before, Hal. Guys on our side selling out. Money, blackmail, warped ideology. It's all the same dirty laundry."

"A traitor is a traitor. The upshot is, the Man agrees. You've got carte blanche to go out there, knock on doors. Or kick them down. Your call."

"How soon?"

"Give me two, three hours maximum to work out travel arrangements, put together the whole intel package for you, what players we can manage to put on your scorecard on our end. And I'll deal with the FBI, the mayor, whoever else is on the warpath, looking to squeeze you and Agent Broadwater. In other words, you're free to go."

"Never a doubt."

"Call me back. It sounds like you've done enough. I'm thinking the cell up there has to be burned down." Brognola paused, waiting for a response. "I hear silence, Striker. I'm thinking my next suggestion to lay low until I get you to JFK is not an option."

"The hit team. It's just a hunch, but one, maybe more of the gunmen got away."

"There has to be a hundred thousand ways to get out of the Big Apple."

"I can't let it go."

"I'm not asking you to. But we're familiar with the drill. There will be no ID, nothing, zip, not the first computer file or document telling us who these guys are. They're black ops, ghosts, like you said. They were created by our side to stay faceless and nameless to do the kind of dirty work that would have the politicians screaming for complete control over the CIA, NSA and every other alphabet-soup agency. These guys are just part of the spook machinery."

"Now a murdering juggernaut gone amok."

"I have to run. Fires to put out and at least one to start."

"I'll be in touch."

"Hopefully from a cab on your way to the airport."

Bolan let that go. No point in causing his friend any more unnecessary stress, as Brognola punched off from his end. The soldier wasn't about to hang around the fort while he suspected a few savages were still on the hunt for innocent blood. With the sat-link back in its hole and locked down, Bolan took the second war bag. The Executioner read the look of more bad news on Broadwater's face as he entered the living room, the FBI man lowering the tac radio.

"One of them just turned up on Seventh Avenue." Broadwater stood, his eyes smoldering with anger. "Two more officers down. Another citizen body count in double digits before the bastard shot his way into a diner and blew himself up."

IN THE TWISTED MIND of the terrorist, Bolan knew he saw no shortage of murderous opportunities, with so many choice targets in a city like New York.

Well, covering all of them was next to impossible, he knew. At roughly the start of rush hour, the mayor had sounded the alert over radio and television, urging New Yorkers—nonessential personnel, he called them—to remain home. That wasn't about to happen, Bolan knew, short of a nuke dropping out of the sky. Tough and determined, attitude to spare was the rule in that town, not the exception. Most New Yorkers, Bolan knew, would march out there, middle-finger salute and all to defy whatever the odds a few maniacs might rear up in their face to snatch it all away.

Which meant teeming streets, normal rush-hour madness, streets jammed with vehicles, sidewalks swollen with foot traffic, restaurants and businesses packed. Just as he found it as they came to a dead stop in snarled traffic in the glass-and-concrete canyon of Midtown.

Broadwater had informed Bolan during the drive across the Brooklyn Bridge that everything short of martial law, meaning troops and tanks and gunships, was descending on all five boroughs. He didn't elaborate, but a tally of all the blue-and-whites and his discerning eye picking out the unmarked units, Bolan found the police hunkered down, scouring their surroundings with an unflinching grim eye, ready to take care of business. And poised, Bolan could be sure, to return a lethal favor or two to any armed wanderers they even suspected were linked to the killers of cops and civilians alike.

Part of the problem the way Bolan saw it was it might prove too little too late. For instance, only now, as rush hour was in full gear, were police setting up checkpoints on both sides of the East River and the Hudson. Uniformed cops were stacking up on subway platforms, Grand Central station, and so on. Security was beefed up on full alert from the Statue of Liberty all the way out to La Guardia, JFK and back to Newark International. Overtime for every beat cop and detective, with the National Guard right then rolling in to set up camp in Queens and Brooklyn.

Broadwater was scowling at the stalled traffic, glancing around, searching for something, anything out of the ordinary. "Has to be a police checkpoint, maybe down Forty-fourth or over on the Avenue of the Americas holding everything up. Only nobody in their right mind drives into Midtown this time of the morning. I guess that's what you're counting on? Somebody not being in their right mind, that is."

"I'm counting on the last of them already dead."

"Yeah, well, just in case...you've got eight million, maybe more like ten million faces in this city, what with the immigrant flow, most of them illegals these days. It's still your show until I drive you out to JFK."

Bolan glanced at the big agent. Broadwater was tugging at the sleeves of his oversize windbreaker with FBI on the back. "Sounds like you're not going to miss me."

Broadwater grunted, gave Bolan what he assumed passed for a friendly smile. "I appreciate your man going to bat for me like you said he would. The brass had a different tone when I checked in last, damn near respectful. Like somebody down your way made them believe their careers and pensions were on the line. Thanks."

"It wasn't your mess. And I couldn't see the point in you catching the heat, acting on my orders, while I fly off into the sunset."

"Decent of you, just the same."

"I would have done it for anybody who backed my play."

"Well, clout or not backing you up from Wonderland, I don't think you want to come back here anytime soon. A few of the guys over me might be the lost spawn of J. Edgar himself, if you get my drift."

"I've seen the type."

"Okay. Beyond sitting in traffic, hoping a crazed shooter or two turns up, any ideas?"

Bolan caught the gist of the man's point. Granted, it was a long shot, plodding around Midtown, searching, hoping for a lucky break, but this was the guts of Manhattan. Like any detective hunting a killer, Bolan tried to put himself in the opposition's head. The rough triangular outline of the Theater, Diamond and Garment Districts between Fifth and Ninth, with Rockefeller Center, various and sundry museums and galleries and Wall Street north, St. Patrick's Cathedral, with the churches of St. Thomas, St. Peter in the vicinity if Muslim fanatics wanted to make a statement...

All of it was way too ripe with easy pickings for any terrorist worth his murderous impulses to pass up. Still, Bolan was starting to think he might just call it off and head for JFK early.

Then the shooting and the screaming hit the air.

A lightning burst of bedlam came from the direction of Forty-fourth where the famed Algonquin Hotel stood, and he believed the Tradesmen Building towered on the same block.

Bolan grabbed up the Uzi, shouldered out the door. A stampede had already begun in the kind of grim earnest that would see victims falling under the mad rush alone, bones breaking or worse. The whole mass of howling pedestrian overflow was a rolling wave of countless bodies surging around the corner, pedestrians already toppling, left or trampled where they fell. Beyond the shouting and wailing, the Executioner clearly heard twin stutters of autofire.

By now stranded commuters were in panic, laying on the horns up and down Fifth Avenue, metal rending next as vehicles attempted to bulldoze any path of escape they could create. A few of the more daring or curious came out of their cars in various states of confusion and fear, then began running in all directions to clear the battle zone. The whole bottleneck of man and machine was about to cost even more lives.

Bolan bounded up on the trunk of a cab, charging ahead, leaping roof to hood, pounding ahead over the vehicular bridge, veering for the stampede. He was flying off the roof of a Mercedes, landing and bulling his own charge through the crazed pedestrian traffic when the autofire and the wailing of wounded or dying victims multiplied in his ears. He knew he was nearly on top of the shooters, and was gathering speed as the rushing mob took him for another mass murderer and leaped out of his path by taking cover in doorways, between parked or stalled vehicles or wherever they thought they could hide and hold on.

There were two of them, as the Executioner gave the pandemonium a search on the run, charging off the sidewalk, weaving between the logjam of vehicles. He was locked in on the shooters, tunnel vision obscuring racing figures and looming structures as nothing but a blur. The reasons why the fanatics had chosen this stop to make their murderous stand Bolan didn't know or care. It was way too much bad luck for too many innocents already that they'd made it this far.

They were splitting up, AK-47s sweeping the dispersing crowds on both sides of the street, then extended bursts of autofire raked immobilized or abandoned vehicles, the lunatics blowing apart glass, stitching a few motorists who were attempting to outrun the tracking storms of lead.

The Executioner hung the Uzi around his shoulder. With innocents scrambling to clear the area or with a noncombatant suddenly popping up at the worst of times, the soldier opted for the steadier and more certain high-velocity punch of the Desert Eagle.

The hand cannon was out and tracking as the warrior dashed up the narrow space between sitting vehicles, heads of noncombatants sliding past his gun sights, whipping into view, there then gone. One heartbeat for a clear shot, the shooter sliding back into the street, and Bolan tapped the trigger. The thunder from the Desert Eagle cut through the brick wall of autofire, horns and screams.

Downrange the shooter took the .44 Magnum round through the sternum, heart blown to mush before a misty burst hit the air on the round's pulverizing exit from between the shoulder blades.

One down.

The soldier was wheeling, Desert Eagle tracking toward the other source of slaughter when he saw the fanatic jerking around in a crazed dance step. Whether mindless rage, adrenaline or both kept him going, the fanatic was holding back on the AK-47's trigger, somehow held it blazing on-line even as crimson spurted from the holes marching over his chest. Bolan squeezed the trigger, dropped him for good with a headshot.

The fury of the howling mob was deafening, as Bolan whipped around, searching for the initial source of gunfire that had riddled the second terrorist. He had a good hunch who had provided the help, but Bolan wasn't prepared for the angry surge, the sick feeling that slammed his gut next.

Broadwater was sliding down the side of a FedEx truck, toppling out of sight.

Bolan jostled and shouldered a charge through a smattering of runners. Rage over this senseless slaughter seemed to obscure his sight with a red film. He was stowing the Desert Eagle, flying around the front end of a vehicle and moving up on the fallen FBI man when a guttural choking drifted through the ringing in Bolan's ears. He was crouching beside Broadwater when a pained smile stretched the FBI man's lips, and he shuddered up on an elbow.

Broadwater touched the holes in his sweater, grimacing, the bottom of the ill-fitting parachute that passed for a jacket touching the street. "Kevlar." He looked up at Bolan. "The wife...she never lets me leave home without it."

12

Wahbat Mazad was on the edge of the couch, rapt but anxious, listening to the gray-haired anchorman.

"As most of you now know this morning in Midtown, Manhattan, the very epicenter of New York itself, was turned into a scene that can only be described as an urban war zone. What we know is that an undetermined number of gunmen opened fire with automatic weapons on crowds of commuters and pedestrians near Fifth Avenue. We believe most of the shooting was right in front of the Tradesmen Building, the, uh, carnage spilling also in front of the famous, long-standing landmark that is the Algonquin Hotel. How many are dead and wounded we do not yet have any confirmed reports, any indication...just a minute. We are receiving confirmed reports now that there were two gunmen. Both of them are dead, whether they were shot by police, or took their own lives, we cannot confirm. This, as you know, comes only one day after the massacre on the F train..."

"It has started. But why have we not received our own call? What is happening, that we would be kept in the dark like this?" asked Yulat.

Mazad didn't have any answers, but he had some clues, vague as they were. The only thing he was sure of right then was the power of his own AKM assault rifle. Yesterday he had received two phone calls from his personal contact in Brooklyn, arranged with Mahlid before they left Iraq, eighteen months ago. According to the leader of the New York cell, one of their own was responsible for what the famous American news anchor was describing as a massacre on the F train.

There was trouble, yes, but Mazad couldn't be positive who was in the most dire straits. Was it his own cell? Or was it their enemy, whom he could only hope and pray was still being hunted in the streets of New York? The special report, which had interrupted their normal afternoon round of soap operas, didn't seem to have much more to offer, at least in terms of rising body counts. Then there was a report about a massive shootout at a Brooklyn restaurant, complete with explosions and dead police officers. The media had run film footage of a burning police helicopter in the middle of Atlantic Avenue, painting the war zone in their usual colorful language and analogies, expressing their shock and outrage, speculating—unconfirmed reports, of course—that an army of international terrorists had invaded the United States.

If they really only knew, he thought.

New York was only the beginning.

But something had gone terribly wrong with the Brooklyn cell, and Mahlid, wording it all very carefully over the phone, had hinted their sponsors may want to pull the plug on their end in New York. Which left a slew of questions tumbling through his mind. Had their brothers-in-jihad in that city been in danger of being eliminated because of the actions of one man since yesterday? Would their sponsors, the Koreans, abandon them there in Chicago? Why hadn't they called, if word had gone out to launch the jihad? Worse, if New York had fallen from grace with the sponsors, then would they come to pay them a personal visit, as in shooting first?

The knock on the door jolted him off the couch. He hissed at Yulat to turn down the TV, then padded for the door. He stared into the peephole, the assault rifle clutched in hands suddenly moist with sweat. His heart was already racing uncontrollably, terrified as he was of finding the hall swarming with police or SWAT, but he felt the pounding in his chest become even more furious now at the sight of the man standing on the other side. He had never seen the face, but why should he recognize the man? Still, there was something in the eyes that warned him.

That was no policeman, which was the good news. But it was the coldness, the lifelessness in the eyes, the way a lizard might view an insect it was about to pounce on for a meal, which made Mazad almost throw open the door and start blasting away. Something, too, about the man in black, standing there, at ease, skin so gray it looked like cigarette ash. And a face with features so sharp, or blunted, he couldn't decide if it was more suited to be on one of those statues he believed was called a gargoyle.

He almost didn't look human. "Who is it?"

No response, then the man bared his teeth in a smile, stepped back and held his arms out by his side, palms shown, as if to say, "What's the problem?"

Mazad drew back from the peephole, waved his assault rifle in an angry gesture for Yulat to hide in the bedroom, the implication clear that he was to come out shooting if this was a raiding party. He unbolted, unclicked and unlatched the series of locks he had installed himself the first week they had rented the apartment. Backing up, he raised the AKM, said, "It's open. Come in."

And he came in, taller and even more whip lean than he'd looked on the other side of the door. More like a reptile in the face and eyes, now that the tiny bubbled peephole wasn't exaggerating the features like the distortion of carnival mirrors.

The man shut the door, reset the locks and bolts when Mazad told him to do so. Mazad had been in the Republican Guard, and he had smelled plenty of death on men, women and children, during the war with the infidels. This man reeked of blood on his hands. He wasn't awash in blood, of course, but Mazad smelled something he could only imagine was akin to a rotting of the soul, evil ingrained into his flesh, past deeds of murder in the eyes, a haunting reminder of a similar future to come. A gray serpent, then, Mazad thought, not to be trusted. He stepped deeper back into the living room, the man actually grinning at the AKM.

"Relax, Wahbat. I come in peace."

The voice was slightly raspy, deep but soft. Controlled, Mazad thought, in a low-key manner—meant to deceive—with an intensity just beneath the surface tone. He found himself both mesmerized and afraid. He couldn't decide if it sounded as if the man mocked the world around him or was prepared to destroy it.

"How do you know my name? Who are you?"

"Just a messenger. Good news or bad news, that's up to you."

"What? Who sent you?"

"Hey, easy with that thing. Guns make me nervous. I'm reaching for a cigarette, okay?"

The slight hump beneath the black leather bomber jacket didn't escape his eye. The man was armed with a pistol. Slowly he took a pack of cigarettes from a pocket, lighting up as he turned that damnable smile on the television.

"I see you've heard the bad news already about your buddies in New York."

"What happened to them?"

Instead of answering, the man looked around the drab apartment with its cracked walls and peeling paint, grunted at the cockroach skittering over the bare wood floor near the couch. "What a dump. I didn't think they'd put you up in a suite at the Hilton, but they could have done a little better than this."

"You are making me very angry!"

"Look at this guy, Wahbat. I've seen that clown before." The man chuckled, again ignoring the question as he shook his head at the television. "Now we've got the expert, the right hand of God himself, coming on to sort it all out for us, the great unwashed. Everybody's an expert these days, like they chat with the Almighty every night or something. Ever notice that, Wahbat? Constitutional law, the stock market, prostate cancer, terrorism. This is a country filled with experts. How do you get a job like that anyway, get paid good money to be a smug know-it-all? Huh?"

Mazad took a threatening step toward the man, then stopped when those dead eyes bored into him. "You talk too much. Answer my question."

"Tell your buddy he can come out of hiding. Both of you need to listen real carefully to what I've been sent to tell you, then somehow pass it on to the others. But watch what you say over the phone. These days, the air itself seems to have ears." He was moving away from the TV, angling for the kitchen.

The rage seemed to roar like a crashing wave in Mazad's ears as the insolent bastard actually went to the refrigerator and opened it. "Feel free to make yourself at home."

"No beer? Oh, I almost forgot. You're Muslim."

He glimpsed Yulat moving into the living room, his own assault rifle aimed toward the kitchen. When the man turned, he dropped the smug comedy act, the eyes turning even colder, if that was possible, Mazad thought.

"We can go for it right here, gentlemen, or you can get those pieces off me and hear me out. Your call."

Mazad snapped at Yulat to lower his weapon.

"By the way, I know Arabic."

Mazad balked, felt the brief quiver in his hands as he let the AKM fall by his side. "What is your message?"

"It's real simple. You are to stay here. You will receive the call you've been waiting for."

"When?"

"Rough time frame? They told me to tell you twelve to eighteen hours."

"And you will sit on us, baby-sit us?"

"I'm leaving—hey, unless one of you goes out for some beer, calls up some whores, I'll throw you a nice going-away party before the jihad starts. No? Well, South Side is not my style. But I'll be close, so will a few others. Watching. Make sure we don't have any more F train situations before the time."

"The Koreans? They are spying on us?"

"Nobody's spying. Just stick to the plan. Do that, then you'll be free to go out there and burn down half this city."

Mazad didn't know what to believe, but he felt the full probing weight of the man's stare, then the stranger smiled, and added, "Jihad, brothers, it's all about jihad. You hang tight, and it's going to be a wonderful day in the neighborhood."

"WHAT THE HELL is this?"

"It's a chopper. A Kiowa JetRanger OH-58, used by both the Army and the Navy, to be exact. Also armed, both minigun and TOW missiles."

"A gunship?"

"A gunship."

Armand Geller was on the verge of adding "you silly bastard," but the DIA man was clearly out of sorts, flailing around, scowling and huffing at the bank of monitors as if a show of antics alone would make the chopper go away. Not the time to antagonize the guy, he decided. Whatever was happening, Geller knew it smacked of trouble.

Turner aimed the dark expression at Geller. "I know what it is. I want to know why it's there."

"One way to find out."

"How's that? We start winging away with the surface-to-air missiles at an Army helicopter?"

Geller stepped up to the control bank, ignoring both the DIA man and the command center assistants—two of his own people, black ops—and stared at the chopper. Flying in from the north, which could mean anything, about two hundred feet up. Slowing now as the pilot cut back on speed, coming in for a closer look at the whole compound. Recon. But why?

"Not quite anything so dramatic," Geller told the DIA man.

Compton, he saw, was working dials and punching buttons on the radio console, looking to cut in on their mystery guest's frequency, ordering the pilot to respond. Their own frequency, so classified not even the Pentagon knew it existed, was courtesy of a FEMA black magic touch. It worked one-way, supposedly, he thought, meaning they could cut into all airwaves, civilian or military, while essentially a firewall was built around their own command channel.

"Then, what?"

Geller waited to hear something from the other side, but his gut told him their company was ignoring the call, making some statement. Not good. Considering the New York situation, he suspected the worst. Somebody had smelled them out. They weren't the only covert act on the block.

The sit-rep Turner had passed on to him earlier, after Bowen had landed in Chicago, was fraught with any number of gloom-and-doom scenarios. Cell Two was on edge, ready to blast out of the gate on its own, until Bowen apparently calmed the troops with a few choice words. Cell Three, he understood, also required a visit by North Korean referees, who reported they strongly suspected that jihad bunch was under an FBI magnifying glass.

"Let's take a ride up there," Geller told Turner. "Polite gesture, get them down on the ground where we can take a closer look."

Geller read the agitation in the DIA man's eyes. Turner might have been stamped by the Department of Defense to officially run the base, the man instrumental in blowing smoke at the right people in Washington, but Geller had long since been sought out by the colonel himself to watch and monitor the whole operation. He caught the flicker of regret in Turner's eyes as he turned back to the monitors, the man probably sinking back in time to the day he bit the hook and was reeled in. Then Geller watched the screens, found the chopper hovering now at the north edge of the compound. Turner would do as he was told. Like the senator, Geller viewed the DIA man as nothing but a trapped rat, in every sense, with his own hand always poised to drown them both if the colonel gave the order. Turner was stuck, all right, the usual vices nailing him to his own cross, the whores, the gambling, trading off a little classified intel here and there for a few dollars more. One of the team, but barely.

Geller moved and took the HK MP-5 subgun off a table. He could almost read Turner's thoughts, the man working his nervous look over the weapon. "Just in case they aren't the reasonable sort, Mr. Turner."

THE PLAN, WAS to go to work immediately on their nerves, start smoking them out using the Justice Department heat at his disposal. In short, the Executioner wanted them to know he was in the neighborhood, while implying when they met he was adding up the score.

Keep it simple. Light a fire.

He was squeezed into the cockpit hatch, looking over Jack Grimaldi's shoulders, the Farm's pilot having just called him in from the troop hold in the belly of the Kiowa. They were hovering now, the soldier confirming, "I see it. Stay afloat, right here."

Bolan watched as the rough equivalent of the Blackhawk SOF MH-60 was lifting off from the helipad in the distance. Coming in for a closer inspection of their visitors or something more heavy-handed? he wondered. He spied three more such gunships grounded near the string of hangars to the distant southwest, a jumble of twin-engine aircraft, two sleek Gulfstreams parked on the tarmac. A control tower rose from the prairie floor, but there was a squat concrete structure that made Bolan wonder what was behind the door. The Farm had antiaircraft batteries concealed in housing similar to what he found there. A reasonable guess, and the spooks on this prairie stretch were likewise capable of taking out any aircraft deemed hostile or suspicious—or whose pilot wouldn't respond to their radio signal. On his order, Grimaldi had shut down the Single-Channel Ground and Airborne Radio System, SINCGARS. Any warning to clear out went unheard and thus unheeded, if that was the message being relayed to them. They weren't quite in the hot zone yet, with missiles streaking to blow them out of the sky, or the chopper wouldn't be on its way. Bolan was also betting they were smart or wily enough, or had plenty to hide, to realize that downing an Army helicopter would only put them under official microscopic examination.

He watched the gunship gaining altitude, nose swinging around, vectoring now, hard and fast their way. He'd seen this particular spook gunship special before. Brognola had stated this wasn't quite a black project, but it was near enough to warrant the classified prototype black gunship, which was basically a cross between an Apache and a Blackhawk, with pylons housing missiles, a minigun in the turret nose.

The compound itself could have the Area 51 conspiracy crowd, Bolan thought, nodding in righteous confirmation they weren't the lunatic fringe fantasizing out loud just to grab their fifteen minutes of fame. Coming in, the soldier had stood in the hatch and found the Farm's satellite imagery on the money. Of course, up close it was larger, more sprawling than pictures snapped from outer space. Under the late-afternoon sun, the main buildings of the complex glittered now, their silver skin made of aluminum or some other alloy, Bolan guessed. West he'd noted the two silver rows of mobile homes, where the workforce was quartered. Then a massive dome just beyond Silver Row, the fenced-in outdoor tennis and basketball courts and Olympic-size pool telling the soldier they weren't strictly all work. A vast motor pool, official government vehicles, mostly SUVs and vans, was situated in a gravel lot that fanned away from what the Farm believed was the main work area. The assumption was that particular mammoth abode doubled as command central, the sweeping stretch of rooftop, prickling with antennae, satellite and radar dishes of various size, a good indicator Aaron Kurtzman had pegged it right.

It had taken a fair amount of time and sweat on Brognola's end, not to mention an exchange of heated dialogue with the FBI to get him to Oklahoma, in the backyard now of what he suspected was a brewing conspiracy. Both the Kiowa and some blacksuits had been waiting for Bolan at the end of his military jaunt from JFK to Tulsa, the gunship requisitioned by Barbara Price, the Farm's mission controller, from an Army ammunition depot south, near McAlester.

Logistical pieces in place, it was once again Bolan's show.

Then there was the ranch house in question. A swift pass over the compound, and Bolan had taken in more government vehicles, a smattering of armed guards outside to keep watch, radar and satellite dishes on the roof.

The whole picture flared up a nagging suspicion in Bolan's gut.

Hinky. All of it.

The blackbird was suspended now, dead ahead, swinging around, the fuselage door thrown open. Two figures wedged themselves in the opening, a big, beefy guy in a cowboy hat gesturing toward the ground. He was clearly bent out of shape. There was a man beside the cowboy, holding an HK MP-5 subgun, and he didn't strike Bolan as the type to restrain himself if the itch to shoot first and ask questions later struck a mood. The soldier had his proved side arms holstered beneath his windbreaker, considered opting for the M-16/M-203 combo in a bin in the fuselage, then decided against tipping any hand where he might need to deliver the knockout blow later.

"Drop us down," the Executioner said as he moved back into the fuselage, waiting in the open hatch. As soon as they touched down, he bounded onto the ground, marched into the rotor wash and found the two men already moving to intercept his course. They pulled up between the choppers.

"Who the hell are you? You have any idea this is private U.S. government property? Do you realize we are authorized to use deadly force against trespassers?"

Bolan slowed his advance, the Justice credentials out and open. He closed the gap to roughly two feet, intent on invading more than just their personal space. "I must have missed the sign on the way in." The gunner, he saw, was dividing the suspicion and anger between the Kiowa and the cowboy. The designated mouthpiece was an odd match, Bolan observed, against both the blacksuit and the space-age dwellings. Cowboy boots, sheepskin coat, with a hip holstered revolver displayed, the cowboy, Bolan saw, held the Stetson on his head as the rotor gust threatened to send it sailing. The smirk was forming on the cowboy's lips when Bolan told him, "Take a good look. This didn't come out of a bubblegum machine." The man peered, grunted, bobbed his head. The other gunner, Bolan glimpsed, was boring the evil eye into him, measuring, thinking dark thoughts, no doubt, and looking twitchy to use the subgun.

Even with the rotor wash it wasn't necessary, as close as they were, but the cowboy was still nearly shouting in Bolan's face. "Okay. So? Special Agent Belasko. That still doesn't give you the authority to trespass on classified U.S. military property."

Bolan put the credentials in his pocket, cut to the meat of it. "I'm part of an ongoing investigation. Kidnapping. So that gives me some latitude."

"Really? All my personnel are present and accounted

for. You took a long flight out here for nothing. Good-bye."

"Thomas Shaw," Bolan said, and that froze them just as they were spinning on their heels. "His wife and daughter were abducted from their home in Middle-burg, Virginia. The man's under contract with the DOD as part of a project here. You people, the way I hear it, are on the cutting edge of Star Wars technology. The Titan Four—ring a bell? The other three of this rocket-brains circle, I'm told, are on this compound. I'm think-ing they might have some ideas. But you can start this mutual cooperation by telling me about Shaw yourself."

The cowboy was dancing now from boot to boot, clearing his throat, glancing at his partner as if he needed help. "Nothing, that's what I'm going to tell you. Whatever happened to Shaw and his family is a matter under investigation by people with a lot more au-thority than the Justice Department."

"Telling me to go home, is that it? It's all under con-trol?" And Bolan tossed it out next, ready to gauge their reaction. "Just like New York."

He thought the cowboy was going to faint, teetering for a dangerous moment, jaw slack, then righting him-self as if it were only the rotor wash threatening to suck him out of his boots. "I think it is best if you go quietly on your way...."

The other guard stepped in, as if to cut off his part-ner before he shot his mouth too much. "Justice De-partment or not, we are authorized to use deadly force."

"So use it."

The hardman chuckled, playing it off, but Bolan could see the dark look passing through his eyes, considering the option. "I trust you'll be on your way and leave this matter to us." He looked at his partner, jerked a nod toward the blackbird, started to turn, then added, "Oh, and if you decide to come back? Make sure you have a little more than some pissant warrant from Washington."

Bingo. Ill will to spare. The challenge was issued, the gunner unable to contain himself from striking the killer pose. It wasn't exactly absolute confirmation of his worst suspicions, but it was close enough, and the Executioner knew human snakes when he saw them.

Bolan stood his ground, watching the rats scurry back for their gunship hole, then turned and retraced his path back into the Kiowa. He told the Grimaldi, "Tulsa. But give me one more look at the ranch house on the way."

"Aye, aye, Striker. You know, those two," Grimaldi called over his shoulder, working them into liftoff, "I've seen more pleasant looks on dead men."

Bolan nodded. "They're dirty. That's why they look dead."

At least, he thought, as far as their souls went. Unless he was way off the mark, and he couldn't remember the last time instinct had let him down, the Executioner had arrived in a viper's nest of traitors.

Soon, very soon, he intended to go out, one with the night, and let the trampling begin.

13

In his experience it was dangerous, bordering on reckless and foolish, to stray too close to the fire of other men's ambition, especially where they sought to conquer and divide those they believed existed only to serve and obey. The obvious question in Armand Geller's mind, then, was who would rule and who serve?

Some of the details for the final conflagration—the Phoenix scenario—were sketchy. However, he knew enough about the running schematics, and he believed he could surely read into the methods and motivations behind the madness of the council's founding fathers to catch a glimpse of the future. When the smoke from their ultimate war finally cleared, he knew whoever was left to rise from the ashes would have grown obscenely rich, with numbered accounts that could buy and sell entire Third World armies. And thus, he believed, enter men's true colors to begin separating wheat from chaff. Human nature being what it was—untrustworthy on a good day—he suspected excessive disposable cash alone would present a series of future dilemmas, potential embarrassments, since at least two among the central core had proved track records of self-indulgence.

What went around, Geller mentally weighed, was a lesson that could prove fatal.

Beyond any glaring peccadilloes among their group, he understood the ultimate goal of seizing absolute power was an extreme hazard by itself. Where they might soon determine who lived and who died—and by the droves, mass murder to them easy as flicking a light switch—it was wise to be wary he wasn't some sacred idol above getting crushed and trampled in the fray if it served their purpose. Hell, they'd even claim his head just for chuckles, he suspected, stroking their monumental egos while mounting one more trophy on their mantel of duplicity and backstabbing. It was a cold reality, holding hands with the devil. And he had seen many men, professionals like himself, who had thrown their lot too close to this particular brand of fire, only to be consumed when it finally burned out of control. And why was it, he wondered, the warriors who did all the dirty work were always the first casualties, deemed expendable when the tide turned or the first whiff of crisis hung in the air?

So there he was, Armand Geller thought, sitting among the gods. Playing the game of life and death right beside them, helping, no less, to pave their rapture to the heavens while the rest of the world would bow, pay homage and beg to be spared from the coming Armageddon of their end game.

There were six of them at the table, seven if he chose to include himself. Something personal, pride, he decided, kept him feeling apart, as different from the rest as heaven was to hell. Not that these six came up short in the ambition and tenacity department; he simply lived on another cosmic plane, a deified mortal in his own right. Beyond the job he'd signed on for, he simply wouldn't count himself among their ranks. Not that he felt unworthy, unclean to be in the presence of men who made much of the intelligence world go-round, eyes to the near future where they planned to send far more than just political and military infrastructures flying off their axis. Far from the bashful sort, the first hint that Geller was being viewed as little more than a monkey to the organ grinders he wouldn't hesitate to speak his mind, or worse if they caught him on an especially bad day. They could dream and scheme all they wanted, even successfully execute unfurling the end game of the Phoenix Council all the way to unleashing the fires of the Apocalypse. But at the first sign their own *Titanic* had sprung a leak, he was guessing—looking ahead himself—that one, maybe two of them would consider abandoning ship, leaving the others to drown. Oh, no mistake, in the event of disaster he would fight to save their mighty ship, professional pride getting the better of him, he reckoned. But if it appeared they would leave him chained to a bag of rocks to go down with the wreckage, he wasn't beyond killing the gift horse.

A full-blown crisis hadn't yet arisen, but an iceberg, he suspected, was right then looming in their path, ready to slice through the hull as the ship tried to stay its course. So far, they'd danced around the one obstacle he was most concerned with, but he sensed a couple of them were building up the courage to broach the subject.

The big guy in black. This Belasko from the Justice

Department. The man who had the stones to fly in unannounced and start asking questions.

Geller leaned back in the barrel swivel chair, peering into the smoke, checking them out one by one through the shroud of white light filtering into the haze, which was contained like choking smog within the walls of the war room. Faces were obscured, but he knew five of the six by voice, shadow and stature. The two men from FEMA, for instance, that murky but almighty Agency that had the power to declare martial law in the event of a national emergency. One of them was retired, but had maintained his old network of contacts, black-ops netherworld connections that were critical to keeping an eye on potential troublemakers in Washington. The other FEMA demigod, still active and so high up the feeding chain it would only take one more "accident" for him to grab the reins of power, was designated as the right hand of the council when the coming storm landed. Then the Chief of counterintelligence from the DIA, Turner's superior, sitting directly across from his counterpart in the NSA, which was counterterrorism. The fifth man he wasn't so sure about, but he had the look of a bruiser, a covert mangler of expendable flesh who knew his way around the wet-work block.

The rumor mill in spookdom, he knew, could churn out any number of wild fabrications, spinning out all manner of doublespeak meant to hide the skeletons, keep friend and foe alike guessing, when more often than not the line between the two was blurred. DOD? CIA? NSA? None of the above? All the above? he wondered. A freelancer, selling his services to the highest bidder? Not even Geller knew who and what the man really was, despite all his cyberspace wizards, the black-ops freelancers at his beck and call. The shady truth was the man was classified, buried so deep from the light of day that even his own mother would deny he'd ever been born.

Whoever the man was, the others, the colonel included, appeared to sit in quiet deference when he'd first called the meeting to order. If Geller wasn't mistaken, one or two of them looked as close to being intimidated by his presence alone—fidgeting some or lighting another cigarette off the butt of a smoke they'd only half-finished—as he'd ever expect to find in the eyes of these carnivores. He could be reading it wrong altogether, but the big man had staked his claim at the head of the table first, then the others took their place. The ceremony, unwritten or performed solely on instinct and respect, struck Geller as equal to lesser Dons waiting on the Godfather's next breath. Even Colonel Chongjin, seated at the other end, watching all of them in his inscrutable way, appeared unusually subdued. Hard to tell, since the only time the man showed any sign of life for as long as Geller had known him was when he bared that smile, which was meant, he supposed, to keep the other guy off balance.

A cloud of cigar smoke hung in front of the bruiser's face as he cleared his throat. When he spoke, everyone listened, Geller finding a couple of them edging forward in their chairs, the voice of God about to come through the cloud. "Gentlemen, I would like to commend you for getting it all this far."

If they took that as a compliment, Geller didn't see

them looking set to raise a toast. The Retired FEMA man worked on his whiskey glass in the silence, while the NSA man was clacking a Zippo, an act that seemed to encourage the DIA man and the active FEMA man to pursue the next round of chain-smoking and whiskey sipping.

Say what he would about a few of them, looking down his nose at perhaps their lack of battlefield experience, but Geller still saw them as old school. It was a no-shit look in their eyes, coupled with what he'd heard them say among themselves in past such gatherings. They were determined to a fault, unyielding in principle to stay their chosen course, unwilling to bow to the changing winds of a world that was passing them by, in all ways. They would stick to their guns, voice their radical opinions in time, some of them sounding extreme to the point of lunacy. But this wasn't some board meeting or congressional hearing, Geller thought, where whatever few dinosaurs left were allowed to waddle around the fort, and only then if they went with the flow.

The silence hung, and the smoke thickened. A particularly mean edge of sarcasm knifed through Geller as he watched them, gathering their thoughts, most likely feeling out the dark edges in each other. He was thinking this was where one of them was supposed to stand and applaud, or bow to the Godfather as a group. There was nothing commendable, admirable or remotely clever about how they had arrived at this juncture. Conspiracies, extortion, the buying and selling of leverage and such were the routine and not the aberration in spookdom. They kept gaining steam and momentum on their rise to the top, winning smiles all around, similar to the defense attorney handing off the weekly envelope bulging with cash in the judge's chambers to get the next verdict in his favor. They kept mounting their own shadow army.

Geller caught the man's narrowed gaze at the end of the table, aimed at him like two pieces of sharp flint inside the smoke cloud.

He went on between puffs of his stogie. "We are down to the wire, gentlemen. But before we proceed, there are a few matters we need to address. As we all know, New York did not fall according to plan. I trust the necessary steps have been taken to correct any such future snags. We are open for discussion."

They had already touched on the night's logistics, but brief reports of the day's events all around seemed to Geller to get glossed over by a sense of urgency building in the room by the minute.

"I have been assured the Chicago cell is contained," the DIA man said. "Regrettably I didn't exercise more control with subordinates."

Geller fought to keep the grin off his face. The buck was being passed to Turner. He could almost see Turner now, ears burning over in command and control, keeping his nerves and paranoia in check as he slipped off to the can for a deep slug from his flask.

"As for the third cell," the man went on, "in brief discussion with the colonel and Turner, I'd say it's fifty-fifty they get blown out of the water."

Chongjin didn't wish to address the matter. Geller glimpsed the colonel as a stone portrait of silent musing.

"Which is why we are moving ahead immediately to initiate," Geller heard the Big Man state. "I agree with the colonel. Unforeseen events have forced us to accelerate the whole process."

The man from NSA spoke up. "Our specialists have warned me there is no absolute undetectable corridor we—or several of us—will take on our way out. Virtually impossible, with satellite passovers, NORAD so close, in fact, although our experts believe there might be a narrow window of opportunity further out for us to pull off our vanishing act. Considering our detail out west isn't scheduled to leave until 2400 hours their time...but given the day's events, I concur that we move immediately on this."

The retired FEMA man killed his drink. He rattled the ice around some, seemed poised to search the room as if a butler would materialize out of the smog, then asked, "How about the schematics?"

The question was directed at the DIA man, who answered, "Blueprints, essential ballistic date, telemetry mathematics and other classified technical data, including X-ray laser systems and the Medusa's web shield layout—all logged on disc."

"Under lock and key, we take it?"

"Good to go on the way out with Turner. I have the access codes to all files."

"I hope they're committed to more than just memory." the big man said.

"Right here in my briefcase, sir."

"And our catch from back east?" the retired FEMA man wanted to know.

The man from DIA checked his watch. "Any time

now. Within the hour, but I will double-check on progress before we leave."

"Colonel?" the big man said.

Geller felt the heat rise a notch as he saw Chongjin stiffen in his seat, glance his way before he took center stage. "I feel it imperative I refresh memories at this late hour, so that we have a full grasp of the immediate future and a clear understanding of all of its meaning to each of us. This is not and has never been simply about one aim, one goal, one man. On either side. The time has come for us to put aside personal philosophies which shape our various end plans. I have heard plenty already about how the face of America is changing for the worse, how in the next generation you dread who might land in your White House."

Geller felt the grunt rolling around in his chest, decided it was time for a cigarette himself, if only to keep his face free of an easy read.

"You have your political puppets, with more appointees guaranteed to join them as our campaign contributions filter their way to Washington. Part of the package of our mutual cooperation," Chongjin stated. "However, Geller can confirm the senator's state of mind, if you choose to ask him."

Geller played it cool, fired up, drew easy on his smoke while waiting out the next round of silence. No one seemed so inclined to inquire about the senator's mental and emotional health, taking it for granted it was under control.

Then Chongjin took him off the hot seat and went on to other matters. "This is about SDI technology, but that is only one item. Our own exchange program, devised by all of us gathered here. Yes, you are giving me this Titan Four, lending me their brains, if you will. With schematics on Medusa, I—we—will soon be in a position to become our own power, dictating world affairs. On our end we already have the basic materials, alloys, rocket fuel, uranium, plutonium, processors and so forth. We also have some of the technical expertise, but nothing close to the four men we will take out of this country.

"Further, the goal, or one of them, will be not only seeking to neutralize and render useless any future so-called Star Wars technology, but we will be build our own SDI net in outer space with satellites we hope to likewise arm with thermonuclear laser-guided warheads. During the entire process, those of us in this room, along with my country, will become a nuclear superpower. A conquering elite. With the army we have recruited and assembled outside the United States, with the various ordnance at their disposal, Washington can and will become nothing short of a slave to our demands. Especially after they get a taste of the anarchy to be unleashed, a look into their future if they do not bend to our will. I will tell you now, in no uncertain terms, this is the hour we are to be at our most resolute, our most determined, our most brave.

"Now, there has been a slight alteration in our immediate plans to initiate."

Geller saw the colonel look down to the far end of the table. The big man picked up the ball, said, "The bulk of nonessential personnel will be left behind, of course. Fortunately there are only two families with children. Once initiation is under way, the ones who will be going will be rounded up."

"The story they will be told is that the base is under attack," the colonel said.

"Attack?" the NSA man inquired. "By whom?"

The colonel showed the smile. "Terrorists." He lifted a hand before inquiring minds started bleating out the confusion. "I am sure they all watch the news. These are not stupid people. It shouldn't be too far beyond the realm of possibility that such a thing is possible. Mind you, resistance will not be tolerated. Turner and two of our operatives have the list of nonessential personnel who won't be making the trip. They will commence initiation once we are finished here."

A bloodbath in the wings, Geller knew, mass execution. A mental scan of civilian numbers, among them engineers, labor and maintenance, cooks, and he guessed a ballpark figure of a hundred bodies, one-fifty tops. Women and children? Roughly a quarter of that.

"We will be flying," the colonel said, "all available aircraft to a designated area inside New Mexico. Recent events, as stated, have forced us to move swiftly, and likewise we have formed a contingency strategy due to circumstances beyond our immediate control. Plan B is for us to fly several of our operatives to a private airfield. From there we will be transported by vehicle to wait for our detail from Nellis."

That was all news to Geller, and judging the NSA man's furrowed brow and the DIA man's quizzical frown, they'd been likewise left in the dark on this tidbit. On top of a sudden shift to this mysterious Plan B, Geller knew all about the recruitment angle, having had a hand in the original hunt for suitable cannon fodder. He briefly considered just how much could now go badly wrong. In the beginning he had voiced several objections when the recruitment was launched, with candidates chosen, for the most part it seemed, solely on the merits of sociopathic tendencies. Well, his input had been ignored, the council bulling ahead, snatching them out of dead-end lives for one last shot at the elusive brass ring, shipping them off to the wild Pacific yonder to become what he could only think of as the council's doomsday soldiers. Killers. Marauders. The recruitment, the whole retraining program alone, bordered on insanity since most of their army had been drummed out of the military. Now mass slaughter of civilians. Jetting off to hole up in New Mexico while Nellis did or didn't make it to the scene. Changing the plan, in short, just as the game was about to start. Why did he feel the sudden urge, he wondered, to interrupt and recite to them Murphy's Law?

The colonel had either said enough on the matter, or handed the ball off again to the big man for further explanation. "It's an underground, abandoned, little-known fallout shelter once used by the Army from the old litmus days of atomic testing."

"A bunker," the man from NSA said.

"More or less," the big man said. "It's where we will wait it out until our ride from Nellis shows up. It's remote enough we're hoping no one will think to give it a thorough search, either from ground, air or outer space. Upshot—it makes for a shorter haul on both ends."

"Which brings me back to the original reason for this change," Chongjin said, and seemed to direct his words to Geller. "New York, it would appear, has nearly thrust us to the very edge of exposure. Does anyone find it remarkable that this superassassin, this Reaper, was the only one who managed to make it out of New York? More, he stated it wasn't the police or SWAT commandos who, in his words, 'mucked his play.' He claims it was one man who sent him running. A nameless adversary who now has a face that appears to match this superassassin's vague description of the individual who flew in to the main compound today. Mr. Geller?"

Geller smoked, took his time, feeling the knife coming his way. "Exactly what are you asking, Colonel?"

"Your opinion. Is this man a special agent from the Justice Department?"

"In my opinion, no."

"Then, what?"

"Covert. Black ops."

"Someone, some agency or covert arm of the military, knows of our existence. And where we are," Chongjin told the group.

Geller felt the chill ripple through the room, the insinuation being someone had talked, jumped to the other side of the tracks.

The NSA man spoke up. "He was checked through by my people when I first got word from you," he said, glancing at DIA. "All the i's are dotted, the t's crossed on this Belasko individual. Ask me, it's too neat a package."

"A front?"

"That would be my guess," the man from NSA told Chongjin.

Geller could feel Chongjin building steam to pursue some line of interrogation, but Geller's pager beeped.

He could almost hear them drawing a collective breath as he felt their stares boring into him. His ops were calling him out to the command and control room, which, Geller knew, signaled an emergency. Excusing himself, he ignored the questioning eyes inside the smog, stabbed out his cigarette and beelined for the double doors. His gut was churning, suspecting what he already knew awaited. Grillo was already moving away from the banks of monitors, but Geller found the problem on the first set of screens. Their equipment was state-of-the-art surveillance and countersurveillance, everything from simple camera detection down to laser beams and infrared scanning that would light up an intruder's face in the dark in living color.

And the guy was filling up the screen. Belasko. Geller bit down the curse, no time for a show of nerves to the troops. He needed to get control of the situation.

"He just rode up," Grillo reported. "Sitting there. Watching us."

Geller glimpsed the shadows, illuminated in white-and-green glows. There was scuffing behind him, and one of Chongjin's five commandos said, "I need to tell the colonel."

"Wait a second. We'll handle this." Geller picked five volunteers on the American team, then told Grillo, "Two vehicles. Go out there and take care of this problem. I don't want to hear another word about this," he added.

Grillo agreed, and Geller watched as they grabbed up assault rifles and subguns, moving out for the motor pool to claim vehicles. "At ease," he told Chongjin's hired guns as they danced a little, exchanging looks.

"What do you have?" he snapped at his radar man, who shook his head. The screens were clear of air traffic. The normal flow of air traffic in and out of Tulsa, of course, but the FAA people were under strict federal guidelines issued them from DOD. Since this was restricted military airspace, routine flights were diverted from this area.

Geller looked back to the screen. The guy sat in his SUV, checking them out. Surely he knew he was being watched. Surely he knew someone would be sent out. Well, it didn't matter now, Geller thought, he could be armed with a presidential directive but that wouldn't help him.

But why was he alone? No gunship in the vicinity now. And why did that bother him? Geller wondered. Who the hell was this guy really?

He could feel the Koreans getting more antsy with each passing second. He told them, "We're ready to pack it up." He wanted to add, "The show must go on." But every shred of instinct earned on the killing fields warned him Belasko was there to crash the party.

THE EXECUTIONER WATCHED the two SUVs pull around the far west edge of the building, headlights flaring on as they angled his way. The structure itself was dark, top to bottom, end to end, leading him to wonder on the drive in across the prairie if they had packed the up place until a scan through his infrared binos turned up a wandering sentry. The armed guard vanished quickly inside the building once Bolan braked the Jeep Cherokee rental, some two hundred yards north of the ranch house, nose and headlights aimed dead ahead at the compound.

The alert had been sounded.

Recalling the gunner's earlier words, Bolan had returned, armed with a lot more than warrants to back his suspicion. The M-16/M-203 combo was ready for action, muzzle up as it was canted against the shotgun seat. The soldier was now weighted down in full combat harness and webbing, ammo pouches stuffed with spare clips, grenades. Both side arms were resting beneath the baggy windbreaker meant to shield the battle works from the eyes of passing motorists or curious highway patrolmen on the ride in from Tulsa. The nylon satchel dumped on the passenger seat was nearly bursting with the mixed party favors of frag, incendiary, flash-stun and buckshot rounds. Both the hand-tossed variety and missiles for the M-203.

Bolan had waited with the Farm's blacksuits at their own restricted area at the airport. Final planning, touching back with Brognola, and Bolan made his decision to come back hard, ready to open the cage door for the savages to come snarling out, show their hand. Night fell, and he left the Farm blacksuits with the Kiowa, a radio call and fifteen minutes, give or take, away, due east on the prairie. Backup in the wings, but Bolan didn't want Grimaldi showing up on radar screens, warning the troops he was moving in before Bolan was close enough to reach out and touch them.

Bolan checked the darkness beyond the coming vehicles, his surroundings, in case the ride out was a diversion to sneak in lethal shadows on foot. Clear all around, it looked, present company excluded. He watched as they pulled up, SUVs, side by side, trailing spools of dust, forty, fifty yards at the most. They tipped their hand, hitting high beams as they braked the vehicles, but Bolan anticipated the blinding lights, squinting away from the harsh beams lancing his face.

Show time.

The Executioner lifted the assault rifle by the muzzle, slipped his hand down to the stock but held it horizontal, out of view, as he opened the door, stepped out. Just in case, on the far reach of suspicion he was wrong, the Executioner intended to give them the last benefit of the doubt. Beyond the hum of his vehicle's engine, he heard doors open, hard-soled feet crunching packed earth. He figured four to a vehicle, eight tops, but his eyes were adjusting to the white shroud now, peering, making out four, then five distinct shadows.

"Belasko," he called out, "Justice Depart—"

He saw it coming, assault rifles and subguns swinging around, muzzles lighting up. The first rounds were drilling his door, punching out the window in a spray of shards when Bolan dived back onto his seat.

War had been declared, and Bolan figured he hadn't come this far to put it in Reverse and race a retreat out of there. He wasn't about to stay put, either, as rounds slammed the windshield, slivers raining down on his face next as the storm of autofire started pounding fist-sized holes in glass.

He was under fire, with a nest of traitors hunkered down and watching what they hoped was a quick execution of a snooping G-man.

Not this night, the soldier thought, and decided to seize back the advantage.

He reached up, dropped the transmission into Drive. It was awkward, but adrenaline settled him into place quickly, as the Executioner squeezed around, low beneath the rounds snapping overhead and slicing off the interior. Bolan took the wheel. To the furious beat of bullets drumming the hull, Bolan floored the gas. When the needle shot up to twenty and climbing, Bolan took the satchel. Hunched low, the M-16 was grasped, ready to go out the door beside him as he maintained an awkward loose hold on the steering wheel to keep the battering ram on course. As slugs kept thudding glass and metal, the startled war cries of armed shadows sounded uncertain in the next heartbeat. It was clear, just the same, they were either holding their ground, firing on, or piling in to get their SUVs out of the onrushing missile's collision course.

Bolan bailed out the door, certain the SUV's momentum would carry it through to create the diversion he sought to get him started. The Executioner took the jarring impact on his shoulder, rolled up and let the M-16 rip free on full-auto to begin trampling the black-ops vipers.

Duplicity, of course, cut both ways.

Beyond the usual charades, the lurking hands of treachery simply came with the turf. Colonel Chongjin wasn't sure what to believe, much less what to expect next. Naturally, long before the orchestration of current events was even on the drawing board to abduct the Titan Four and fly them out of America, his mind had been firmly set to not trust his counterparts; he barely trusted his own people to follow this through to its conclusion.

Chongjin begrudged it was a new age, especially with the coming future of supertechnology looming just over the horizon. The kind of power that, if he didn't obtain it now, would leave his country lagging far behind the competition. His countrymen would keep starving, denied any economic opportunity that came with production and flourishing of cutting-edge technology, would remain mired in what he could only best describe as Stone Age. Not that he especially cared, one way or another, if entire herds of simple-minded rice farmers lived or died, but there was his own bottom line to consider—the dream of ousting Kim Jong Il, and he would require as much peasant backing and approval as he could tolerate. In time, he told himself, it would happen, but only if all went well in the present, people carried out their duties and responsibilities, lived up to their end of the bargain.

A coup d'état to seize the reins of power had joined him with old rivals. It was a strange coalition, indeed, he thought. Chongjin knew these men by rank, stature, deeds. Basically they had willingly turned their backs on their country and their constitutional duty out of primal hunger for absolute power, to create a new America as they saw it. The bottom line, or so they claimed, was to disrupt and shatter the infrastructure of American society so the eventual endgame was a nightmare beyond imagination. These men envisioned anarchy, spoke openly of how terrified masses of armed citizens would take to the streets when the frenzied civilian populace realized a military regime from hell had landed among them. That what most Americans cherished— money and jobs, surrounding themselves with all the creature comforts and toys of privilege, the future bright with promise for the children—was about to be no more. Enter FEMA. Exit law and order as the final flaming vestige of democracy. The American dream dead. Next the other members of the council would restore order— their order—and their martial law implemented by ruthless legions of former U.S. military men, with a smattering of felons tossed into the savage mix, recruited over the past two years or so. There was much more to the bigger picture, he knew, including the terms of peace they'd put to their government, the method of extortion, or the vow of punishment for resistance and disobedience as they took down the palace—the White House and the Pentagon for starters.

A number of dark thoughts kept boiling to mind as he half listened to the council hashing over the situation in New York, debating the merits of what their superassassin had passed on to them about his encounter with the unknown, as if mere speculation would help them solve the riddle. Geller came as close as he would dare to trusting any of them. The colonel had met Geller while both of them were counterintelligence operatives in South Korea, rumor having it Geller was perhaps for sale if the price was right. The abduction scheme had its humble origins in a simple cash transaction, where Chongjin had reached a conclusion—after Geller eliminated a few of his own operatives—that both their sides had mutual goals, ending primarily in a search for power. Geller knew of like-minded men, introductions eventually made, details and dreams...

Ancient history, he decided.

What was the ruckus? Shooting out back? Had a small army of American covert operatives come to storm the place? Chongjin knew his own men wouldn't hesitate to barge through the door, armed and prepared to die to make sure he found safe passage from there.

At the sound of the first shots, a sense of urgency, even an air of panic, seemed to find its way into the smog. The colonel was rising, thinking it best to end the meeting and begin the initiation when the explosion occurred.

Chongjin nearly jumped out of his seat. The explosion was coming from somewhere out back, but close enough, it seemed, to shake the walls. He knew any heavy ordnance, grenades, rocket launchers and such were stored back at the main complex. If not their people, then who?

The stampede outside the doors, the sound of boots pounding wood, men scrambling all over the place, deepened his anxiety. They were shouting now, voices competing to try to fathom what was happening. Chongjin was out of his seat, wheeling toward the commotion, when the doors flew open and he found Yuk Kim, wild-eyed and rattling on about an intruder on the way. One man? Nonsense! Impossible!

Chongjin whirled as the other council members prepared for flight, chair legs scraping, breathing heavy. The DIA man stood, nearly pitched in sudden haste, his foot catching the chair, when Chongjin barked at him, "The briefcase!"

The colonel was leading the exodus for the doors, the sound of weapons stuttering on as their people ran down the hall leading out back, hope coming alive in his heart that whoever was attacking them was soon to be extinct when the explosion ripped through the heart of the ops center. The blast was so close, fire and smoke in his face, some wet object slashing off his skull, the wrecking ball of shock waves bowled him down.

THE EXECUTIONER'S SUV missile was a home run, a head-on collision that bought him precious heartbeats. His enemies were torn between scrambling to get out of path of the runaway bulldozer or searching him out to resume firing. The Executioner expected at least two or three gunners to come into sight from the other side as his metallic rhino rumbled past them.

Anticipation paid off.

Bolan was already on his feet, M-16 up and shooting from the hip, the soldier milking short precision bursts across their chests. Two shadows spun, dropping in their tracks.

They had called the killing play, so the Executioner decided not to disappoint the opposition, much less waste one second that could find him out in the open, exposed to return fire. The SUV's impact had shot glass through the air. One of men howled briefly as glass slashed his face.

Bolan tapped the M-203's trigger, and blew the three survivors into flying broken mannequins, sent them sailing from the fireball shredding apart their SUV, screams trailing away into the night.

With the grenade satchel around his shoulder, Bolan parted the Velcro straps and opened it for quick delves, the 40 mm rounds already marked according to their particular wallop. The Executioner marched ahead, spotted a mangled form, right leg missing below the knee, crawling beneath the umbrella of firelight, and treated the moaning snake to a mercy burst of autofire.

All done there, he found, and the Executioner jogged past the hungry flames, his sights laser-focused on the command center. Bolan was beyond anger, forging on, cold to the core. Still, someone inside had marched the first round of hitters out to take him down, all hands thinking they had little more than a lamb waiting to be slaughtered. A hundred yards and bearing down, the soldier was on the way in to shoot and blast out the very heart of the rat's nest. The Executioner stole a moment to load the M-203 with an HE round, then drew target acquisition on what he guessed was a large bay or observation window beside the double doors.

A few shadows came running now, just as the soldier triggered the launcher, pumped the missile through the targeted window. The ensuing thunderclap pealed from the other side of the building. The round must have flown unimpeded until the impact fuse slammed into resistance. If there was any lingering doubt left he sent another HE hellbomb on its way for the shadows venturing a few ungainly steps into the unknown. They were professionals, though, he was sure, backed by training, experience and maybe the blood of past victories on their hands. Flight or even retreat was clearly not an option in their minds. They were on the verge of splitting up to make themselves less available targets.

Too late.

And more casualties were snapped up by oblivion as the HE round was dumped into the heart of the shadows.

Bolan reloaded the M-203's chute again with another HE pulverizer, and sent it streaking through a narrow doorway. A thunderclap was followed by a brilliant saffron flash from inside the belly of the nest. It was clear he had their undivided attention now, as the din of voices raised in panic reached his ears.

Bolan figured he had a few seconds to burn while they reeled about in the smoke, survivors scraping themselves up off the floor, he imagined, digging themselves out of wreckage. And opting, most likely, for an exodus out the front for the motor pool.

Not so fast.

The Executioner slipped an incendiary missile down the M-203's snout. A brief scouting of the building's corners, clear of blacksuit traffic, and Bolan decided it was time to burn the down whole viper's nest.

The Executioner slowed his jaunt, raised the assault rifle and sent the fire starter winging for a second-story window.

THE CALL TO ARMS, an instinctive urge to retaliate, to save the night, had spared Geller from the first explosion in the command center. He was halfway up the stairs, HK MP-5 subgun leading the ascent, when several of his people bolted down the hall, charging past him to assist their comrades outside. One of Chongjin's henchmen thrust himself into the war room's doorway, bellowing the alarm in his native tongue when Geller had caught sight of the flaming tail streaking past in the corner of his eye. Whatever it was, he knew it was the worst of more bad news on the way, so he hugged the wall, covering his head as the world blew up below him.

Being a little smarter, tougher than the rest, his worst suspicions were all but confirmed. The guy—whoever he was—was no G-man, far from it, but he'd already guessed as much. Geller wanted to kick himself for marching five good ops to their doom. One man, no less. How could this be? How hard a killing task to nail one man, no matter how good, how big or titanium hard the professional stones?

He should have known better. He'd seen the guy earlier, looked into eyes—mirrors of the soul—that wanted to warn him this Belasko was every bit the stone-cold killer he was. Pride, he guessed, had gotten the better of judgment.

One more step up, he glanced back, unable to pry his

eyes off the destruction he was rising above for a long, dangerous moment, hacking out the grit that swirled up, choking his senses. Unbelievable, he thought. Seven figures worth of cutting-edge countersurveillance equipment up in smoke and flames, the very guts of the command center ripped out in the blink of an eye, ruins now laced with dancing sparks like the fading encore of a fireworks show. Beyond that, he figured at least three more of his own were down, somewhere below in the hall. Hard to tell with all the smoke, a severed limb turning up, here and there, in the whole mass of devastation. One of Chongjin's gunmen, he spotted, had taken the rocket ride across the room with the blast, kicked into the bay window where he now sprawled over the sill, wedged in the jagged shards. They were staggering from the war room next, frantic voices he recognized calling out for assistance. Incredible, but Geller then found four of the Koreans and a matching number of his men had somehow cleared ground zero, figures rising from the deepest corners to begin a slow march through the smoke. It wasn't hard for Geller to figure where the council was going next. Chongjin and company were bailing.

Geller left them to their flight.

Go! he urged himself.

Something burned deep inside Geller, and it went way beyond pride. Even though it bucked traditional cold professional logic, this had just turned personal. The sleeping quarters, he knew, were upstairs, windows that looked out to the north. From there, he could take up a sniper's roost, assuming of course, the bastard was still an available target.

Another blast, more screams, then gone, spiked his senses. He felt his teeth grinding together, a red film squeezing into sight as hot rage shot the blood pressure up to where his brain started pulsing against his skull. He was nearly topping out when the next thunderball seemed to roar up directly below. A scorching heat shot up to envelop him before the stairs were yanked away by the explosion, vanishing behind groaning wood and billows of smoke. He was falling when a storm of debris flew up, slamming off his head to douse the lights.

THE EXECUTIONER, tuned to every sound and sight, waded into the rubble and the slaughter. The M-16 already fed a fresh clip, another HE round dropped into the launcher's tube and ready to fly, Bolan had the scent of enemy blood in his nose.

He was close now, moving up on their rear, and ready to clobber any survivors with the knockout punch.

Finish it.

The Executioner heard the frenetic shouts of men in flight, well beyond the piled wreckage, shrouded by gray walls of smoke and cordite. He peered at the sprawled forms, checking for signs of life, poised for some blacksuited Lazarus to rise from the carnage.

Not a groan, not a twitch.

It was treacherous, slow going, just the same, threading his advance between mounds of wreckage, stooping to clear the gnawed edges of hanging beams. The incendiary blaze was already hard at work upstairs, eating it up room by room, moments from bringing down the roof.

The Executioner gathered steam, spying the last of

them charging out the hole in front where his HE round had done a fair amount of renovation. Senses, instinct reaching out beyond the crackle of fire, and the soldier had to believe any live ones were on the way out.

Time to help them.

The Executioner fanned the destruction with his assault rifle, scoping out the few strewed bodies for signs of clinging life.

Nothing.

Bolan caught the shouting out front, a babble of English and an Asian tongue that wanted to strike a memory chord....

Korean.

So be it. Hardly any comfort, that prior suspicion now became dark truth.

The heat from up top reached down suddenly, an angry wave pounding the soldier in the back, drawing sweat, urging him on as Bolan rolled through the vandalized hole. He got his bearings a heartbeat later. A van, sprouting antennae similar to what he'd seen in New York, was pulling out, leaving on behind a cloud of dust. How many were left to bail it was near impossible to say, but it didn't matter now.

Walking wounded or not, they were going down for the count.

Doors were slamming, tires spinning, maybe a half-dozen gunmen trailing two suits, a couple of the lords and masters of the conspiracy, he reckoned, the hardforce protecting their rear. Just as Bolan slid past a support column, sights settling on the van, one of the hardmen took that moment to claim the spotlight.

The Korean shooter whipped around, as if sensing or

anticipating the next avalanche of doom set to drop on his back. He was hitting the trigger on his subgun, two or three rounds slicing off the column, but the Executioner beat him to it with a pinpoint stitching up the torso.

Again the soldier had their undivided attention, hardmen whirling, jerking away from their falling comrade as if his death was some contaminating omen. Bolan had no time to spare trading fire. He caressed the M-203's trigger. The round took its wobbling flight for the sitting SUV just behind the hardforce. Two of them stopped firing, eyes going wide as they saw doomsday streaking for them, and bolted a heartbeat before the 40 mm grenade hammered home in a deafening peal. Bodies were sailing, runners toppling from the shock waves reaching out from the motor pool. A quick search in the distance, and Bolan found the van and another SUV swallowed up by darkness.

Three bloodied moaners could wait a moment, their senses pulverized as they crawled from the flaming wreckage. The engine of another SUV was gunning to life on the far left edge of the motor pool when Bolan filled the M-203 with another HE round. It had the usual dark-tinted glass, hiding the numbers inside, but the Executioner knew any crushing of the smallest force, even down to the loneliest number, was no wasted effort.

Bolan sent the HE bomb flying, then the Executioner moved on, hunting the vipers who had wriggled out of the net.

THE SHADOW OF DEATH, Geller found, had passed him by. He wanted to believe this was his lucky night, but he was gagging, sucking air into starved lungs getting seared by all the heat and grit swelling his chest. As the fog cleared in his sight, tasting the bittersweet flow of blood in his mouth, he made out the next round of shooting, and yet another explosion. It was out front, he knew, as the sound and fury filtered into his ringing ears. He kicked out at the shards that had buried him. It took a full second, but he realized he had somehow kept a grip on the subgun. Miracle of miracles, but there was no sense in questioning any good fortune on this night.

Belasko, he knew, was out front. Another explosion—how many grenades had the bastard dumped on them already?—thundered from the direction of the motor pool.

Enough.

One way or another, Geller was bent on ending it. Besides, pride had him by the short hairs, and he knew he couldn't stomach living one more minute in this world, tasting the gall of this savage drubbing.

It took every ounce of angry will at his command, but he choked down the fit of coughing, kept the noise of his stagger through the litter of glass and shards to the barest minimum. The bastard seemed to have that second sight, eyes in the back of his head, the closest thing to a psychic gift Geller knew experienced killers and soldiers with ten lifetimes of combat behind them were bestowed with.

He focused on the next round of shooting, which seemed to spill out in a direction farther from the front of the house. Cautiously he squeezed through the gaping maw, across the porch, then heard the sharp grunts coming from the motor pool.

Belasko.

His heart raced, but this wasn't the moment to smile. Not yet. His adversary's back was turned to him. Geller watched, unable to comprehend his own moment of triumph was right there, thirty feet away. Victory dumped by fate in his lap. Belasko was rolling on, the shadow of death itself, over the fallen wounded, triggering mercy bursts into their chests, acting oblivious to the firestorm sweeping out over the other vehicles.

A wave of noxious smells swelled his nose, everything from blood and emptied bowels to burning fuel, but Geller crept an inch or so forward, the bitter stench merely fuel for his determination. This was it. The shadow of death, back to him still, might as well draw a bull's-eye between the shoulder blades, the man even in the act of changing magazines, searching the firestorm for live ones. Geller lifted the SMG, locked his sights for a burst up the spine and took up slack on the trigger.

MACK BOLAN FELT the ice creep up his spine. Then the hair stood on the back of his neck, danger registered, the double whammy alerting the Executioner something was wrong.

In a flash the HK MP-5 subgun sliced its sound and fury through the fire devouring more of the motor pool when Bolan shoved himself ahead, his M-16 sweeping around as the 9 mm rounds scalded the exposed flesh of his neck.

The Executioner was clearing the fire when a ruptured fuel tank was sparked off, an SUV bursting apart and spewing gas, with winged debris impaling into an engine hood, the roiling black clouds enveloping the vehicle. Bolan absorbed bites of shrapnel on the shoulders and back, blistering heat in his face, but the whole commotion of shooting wreckage and his bolt ahead allowed him to clear the tracking autofire by an eye blink, as he likewise propelled himself a few paces from the incinerating touch of the blast.

The hardman made the adjustment next, lining him up with the SMG, when the Executioner held back on the trigger of his assault rifle, shooting from the hip. Even with features plastered in blood painting, Bolan knew those eyes, matched them to the blacksuit who made the threatening noise when his Kiowa JetRanger had touched down earlier at the main compound. The Executioner ducked from the hail of bullets, the gunner's SMG jumping around next as Bolan hit him with a rising burst of autofire. Starting low, not leaving anything to chance, Bolan opened him up, crotch to throat, a straight chopping line, pinning the shooter to a support column, a lurching crucifixion in progress. The guy held on, still firing the subgun in a one-handed pose. Another burst of 5.56 mm rounds to the head, and the Executioner sent him toppling.

The Executioner gave the killing grounds a thorough scouting. The same fire that had saved him was well on its way to consuming any savages who might stir for a break out of the blaze. The walls caved in, the roof was coming down in a jettison of sparks, smoke balloons rising for the sky.

No live ones within or beyond the ring of fire around the motor pool.

Check.

No point in belaboring the oversight now, having

missed a shooter on the way out the front door. It was a rare moment, even under combat stress, when Bolan didn't drop and put down for good his target or left his back exposed. Perfection in any arena was a common human goal, unattainable, to be sure, usually driven, consciously or otherwise, by ego and ambition. But anything short of perfect in Bolan's world meant no second chances to get it right.

The Executioner discovered just how imperfect a world it was when he grabbed at empty space where his tac radio used to hang. He must have lost it on his dive out the door of the SUV rental during the bull charge against the first group of gunners. Possibly shot off his hip, or simply left it behind in the SUV when he'd come under fire. Moot point, no time to spare, backtracking, combing the area. Scratch air support or any form of backup.

Alone again.

And the war was just beginning.

* * * * *

The heartstopping action continues
in The Executioner 285,

FINAL STRIKE
Book II of
THE DOOMSDAY TRILOGY

available July 2002

James Axler
Outlanders®

DRAGONEYE

Deep inside the moon two ancient beings live on—the sole
survivors of two mighty races whose battle to rule earth and
mankind is poised to end after millennia of struggle and subterfuge.
Now, in a final conflict, they are prepared to unleash a blood
sacrifice of truly monstrous proportions, a heaven-shaking
Armageddon that will obliterate earth and its solar system. At last
Kane, Grant and Brigid Baptiste will confront the true architects
of mankind: their creators…and now, ultimately, their destroyers.

In the Outlands, the shocking truth is humanity's last hope.

Or order your copy now by sending your name, address, zip or postal code, along with
a check or money order (please do not send cash) for $5.99 for each book ordered
($6.99 in Canada), plus 75¢ postage and handling ($1.00 in Canada), payable to Gold
Eagle Books, to:

In the U.S.	In Canada
Gold Eagle Books	Gold Eagle Books
3010 Walden Avenue	P.O. Box 636
P.O. Box 9077	Fort Erie, Ontario
Buffalo, NY 14269-9077	L2A 5X3

GOLD
EAGLE®

Please specify book title with your order.
Canadian residents add applicable federal and provincial taxes.

GOUT22

DEATH LANDS.

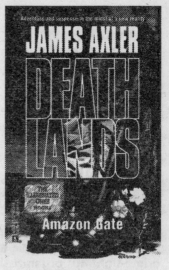

Adventure and suspense in the midst of a new reality

JAMES AXLER

DEATH LANDS

Amazon Gate

Amazon Gate

Available in
September 2002
at your favorite retail outlet.

In the radiation-blasted heart of the Northwest, Ryan and his companions form a tenuous alliance with a society of women warriors in what may be the stunning culmination of their quest. After years of searching, they have found the gateway belonging to the pre-dark cabal known as the Illuminated Ones—and perhaps their one chance to reclaim the future from the jaws of madness. But they must confront its deadly guardians: what is left of the constitutional government of the United States of America.